THE THIN

By the same author

The Honey Plain
Sleight of Hand

ELIZABETH WASSELL
The Thing He Loves

BRANDON

A Brandon Original Paperback

First published in 2001 by
Brandon
an imprint of Mount Eagle Publications
Dingle, Co. Kerry, Ireland

10 9 8 7 6 5 4 3 2 1

ISBN 0 86322 290 0

Cover design: id communications, Tralee
Typesetting by Red Barn Publishing, Skeagh, Skibbereen
Printed by The Guernsey Press Ltd, Channel Islands

For Ruth Benn Wassell
July 1923–July 2000
In Memoriam

"If it has been believed hitherto that the human shadow was the source of all evil, it can now be ascertained on closer investigation that the unconscious man, that is, his shadow, does not consist only of morally reprehensible tendencies, but also displays a number of good qualities, such as normal instincts, appropriate reactions, realistic insights, creative impulses, etc."

C. G. Jung
Aion

"In the destructive element immerse. . . that was the way."
Joseph Conrad
Lord Jim

Prologue

1973

HIS PARENTS WERE spiders at the centre of a bright web. That was how he saw them, sombre, huddled, yet surrounded by brightness: gleaming floors, gilded furniture, a precious painting in the dining room of two Dutch farmers labouring under a rain-rinsed sky.

So the bright filaments flared out from them, though they themselves were dark. His mother had a way of washing her hands dryly. She told him that her hair had once been a deep brown, but she had gone grey early, as early as his birth, and now she coloured it black, a heavy lifeless black, and the clothes she favoured were black. As for his father. . .

They were rich. He knew this, but, of course, when he was a child it simply felt normal. They had lived in New York, on Fifth Avenue, in that bright apartment with its glowing furniture and airy lamplit spaces, with servants who moved softly from room to room – Nanny, Simone the cook, Dorothy the maid – but every summer they went to Ireland, which his mother still called "home". He had two older sisters, Maeve and Alexandra. His own name was Gabriel Charles Phillips.

When he was four years old, one summer day in Ireland, he followed some older children into a copse. They were hurrying on ahead, their laughter disappearing, and he stumbled after them, through whorls of bramble, through a golden density of gorse, through tangled darkness, over a pelt of bracken. He heard a chant in his head: *Don't leave me behind.*

He toppled suddenly, his cheek striking the ground, in his nostrils its smell of loam and rain. He lay there a minute, then hoisted himself up, looking at his hands which were palm down on the black earth, white fingers splayed. Slowly he lifted his left hand and saw a thick black thorn in the middle of the palm, a wound deep and clean as though he had been pierced by quicksilver. He felt no pain, but there was a kind of lightness in his head, a sense of wonder; so perfect it was, that gleaming black thorn in the cushion of his innocent hand, and all around him the mysterious smells of humus and decay. Slowly a door opened in his head and he saw a dark room and his father's face, and there was a smell of blood in this memory and another, even more terrifying smell. For a moment he felt an anguish beyond words. Then the feeling was gone, and he was merely gazing in astonishment at the thorn in his palm. He plucked it out, blood bubbled up, and only then did he cry.

A few years afterwards, in school, he learnt the word *stigmata* and wondered was that day in the copse a sign?

His father, Matthew Phillips, was a tall, grey-haired man. Gabriel himself was dark, with his mother's dark hair and high colour, but he had inherited his father's grey eyes, which were utterly grey, like smoke or the breast of a pigeon, untinctured by blue or green. His mother's eyes were brown, but she had given him her lashes, long, glossy and black, as well as the shape of her eyes, two wide perfect delicate almonds.

Once, when he was thirteen, Gabriel heard two ladies talking in a restaurant. They were glancing over at Gabriel and his family, who were eating dinner at a neighbouring table. Gabriel knew that his family was handsome, that when they appeared in public they sometimes attracted admiring or envious glances. There was his mother with her upswept black hair and imperiously tilted head, his sister Maeve with her willowy figure and slightly haughty smile, his sister Alexandra who was darkly beautiful, like himself. And his father, sternly elegant, well-dressed, taut with energy and intelligence. Whatever might happen behind the scenes, in the dead of night, in their lavish rooms, the family was impressive in public.

This particular evening, Gabriel was positioned in such a way that he could hear the voices of the two women. It was a Sunday evening, when the prosperous families of Park and Fifth Avenues gave their cooks the night off and dined at one or other of the sedate local restaurants, not for a sumptuous meal, but a reliable one, served by seasoned waiters who knew their clientele and catered to all their dietary whims. For instance, there was a very old, very ugly lady who always dined alone, wearing a lot of bulky, uncomfortable-looking clothes, and who invariably took a *whole fish* for her main course, a silver body flopping over the plate, its clouded eye gazing up at her. And there was another family, remote friends of Gabriel's family, in which the children were listless and silent, the husband obviously bored and the wife for ever on some kind of slimming regimen. Although she was bone-thin, she would consult the waiters anxiously – *Is there oil in this? Is that fried? Please don't put dressing on my salad* – while the children sighed and the husband stared with stony indifference over all their heads. Gabriel's mother said that the husband would prefer to be with his mistress, but that since Sunday was Family Night Out, he was obliged to suffer the torpor of his children and the flutterings of his emaciated spouse, who could not understand, the fool, that dieting would not restore her husband to her.

When Gabriel overheard the two ladies, he was plucking with his fork at his grilled sole and wondering about his mother's waspish comments. Although he was only thirteen, he knew what *mistress* meant, because his parents often talked openly about domestic arrangements and domestic betrayals, sometimes with a cynical relish which made Gabriel uneasy, made him wonder what his mother and father themselves got up to. As far as he could see, they never talked about affection, or love. And, despite his youth, he was sensitive enough to observe a coarseness, a lowness, in their manner, when they discussed the pecadilloes of their friends: how their eyes would gleam, how they would laugh a particularly rich laugh, how an intimacy would spring up between them which was absent at other times, as though dissecting other people's sex lives was for them the equivalent of sex.

Gabriel was thinking these things and nibbling at his food when his attention was caught by one of the ladies at the next table. "Celia Phillips," she murmured. This was his mother's

name. He glanced up and regarded his family, but his sisters
were whispering to each other and laughing, and his parents
still discussing the scrawny lady and her bored husband. No
one had overheard the woman but himself.

The same lady continued, "My husband knows all about
Matthew Phillips. *Everything.*"

Gabriel discovered that if he tilted his head slightly he could
observe the ladies. They were about his parents' age, and both
bore the look that he would for ever associate with Park Avenue
hostesses: a certain lacquered hardness, a cold elegance. Their
platinum-coloured hair was impressively coiffed, and their ears
and wrists gleamed with gold. They were dressed in suits and
white blouses, and, like the anxious wife of the weary husband,
both were too thin.

The second lady extended a hand, withered slightly from
excessive dieting, and grasped her wineglass. "People say he's an
absolute *tiger* in the courtroom."

"I *know*. And *not* particularly scrupulous either. But Nicole
has been to their dinner parties, and *she* says that when
Matthew is at home he's *totally* at Celia's mercy. You know how
it is. Confident as hell until he's in through the door, and then
she's got him wrapped around her finger. Humiliates him,
taunts him, that whole castrating thing."

"She looks the manipulative type. It probably makes him
even more of an aggressive bastard as a lawyer. Wouldn't you
say he probably goes *wild, in every way*, once he's out of her
clutches? A tiger in the courtroom and in the – you know."

They laughed. The first lady said something too softly for
Gabriel to hear. Then the second replied, in a new trilling

voice, "She *chooses* them for him? Clever, clever. Well, he *is* glamorous. Did you read the article in–"

"Gabriel," rebuked his mother suddenly, "Stop messing about with your dinner. Eat your fish before it gets cold."

"Gabriel is having one of his humours," said Maeve, the elder of his sisters, with a cruel smile. Gabriel already understood that Maeve was cruel as well as conceited. But she was also impressive, with her shrewdness, her poise. Even though she was barely eighteen, she had got her name and face in the social columns, for attending a ball where she was the only young girl present, in a simple black dress, yellow hair flowing over sun-browned shoulders. Self-assured and radiant, she had been admired by the men at this ball – politicians, magnates, bankers, diplomats – who had neglected their bedizened wives to dance with her. Afterwards, at home, she had described those besotted, absurd old men to her mother, and they had laughed. And Gabriel, listening, had also laughed, for he too admired his sister, despite her cruelty, because she was so much more confident than he was.

Basically, he tilted in and out of their way of life. He realised that Matthew, Celia and Maeve resided in a world where money and position determined nearly everything. They lived luxuriously, but it was also as though they hissed and growled through a jungle, expecting to eat or be eaten. Their luxury was comfortless: it could not protect them from the marauding beasts around them or from their own beastliness. His mother's ungentle observations, the ritual punishments inflicted on him by his father, these things did not surprise Gabriel. He had grown up in his parents' world of outward refinements – fine plate and pictures, a library full of leather-bound books – and inward savagery. But he was not entirely *of* his family.

All his young life he'd had two recurring dreams. In the first, a man with a gaunt face is pursuing him through a dark house. Gabriel knows, in his deep heart, that there is no escape; the strange man will catch him and do things to him. Still he tries to flee, stumbling along dim corridors. In the second nightmare, he and his favourite sister Alexandra walk into their parents' bedroom and discover that it is full of a seething darkness. When they switch on the light, they are confronted with a bedful of snakes, and no parents to be found.

Whatever these nightmares might mean, Gabriel also loved his parents and coveted, perhaps more than anything else in life, his father's approval. Now he smiled across the restaurant table at his father, who met his eyes and said something so startling, so unexpectedly hurtful, Gabriel continued smiling after the words were uttered, as though they had bypassed the smile, leaving it intact, while searing him to the bone.

What his father said was, "The boy's eyelashes are too long. He looks like a girl. Perhaps he *is* a girl. I've never seen much manliness in him. What do you think?" And he invited his wife and daughters to reply.

Alex ventured, "It's not his fault. Maybe Mother shouldn't try her jewellery on him. She puts her necklaces round his throat to see how they look. Maybe Mother shouldn't ask Gabriel to be her model."

"I *see*," Matthew said with his mechanical bright smile, "Ah, I *see*. Celia, my dear, are you *emasculating* my son? Is that what you are up to, darling Celia?"

"Nonsense," she answered briskly. "Don't be such an idiot. He's a perfectly normal boy." She gave Gabriel a warm look, for which he felt grateful. "And he's terribly handsome. Some day all the girls will be swooning over him and making his poor old mother jealous." She smiled at him again, fluttering her lashes (those ultra-long and humiliating lashes). Then, in a harsh voice, she continued, "Sometimes I can't believe the rubbish you talk, Matthew. And do eat up your dinner. I don't want to languish in this boring restaurant all night."

Gabriel wondered if the ladies at the next table had overheard this embarrassing exchange. He thought not. His family knew to speak softly in public and to smile, even when they were throwing harpoons at one another. Anyone observing them would think they were relaxing over a pleasant meal and laughing together. Indeed, the smile he had originally offered his father was still plastered on his face; it was beginning to make his cheeks ache. And his father, though his wife had just rebuked him, was also smiling.

They were changing the subject, thank God. Alexandra – who had championed him, although it would not be prudent to thank her until later – was describing a boy in her class at school. Gabriel pretended to listen, but he was beginning to retreat into his private world, which he had discovered a few months ago, one Sunday at dawn. Still in pain from the thrashing he had received the night before, he had lain open-eyed in his bed, listening to the squeaks and sighs from other rooms, as though the whole apartment were an animal moving in sleep. Suddenly he had realised that one day he would be great, a great artist, like those in his favourite book, an illustrated volume on the lives of the Italian painters by some-one called Vasari. And this thought was so consoling, he had felt as though he were literally aglow, as though the light flow-ing in through his curtains had entered his heart. Over the months, that first incandescent thought had flowered into a series of fantasies. At this moment, he was imagining that he was at a party in the Metropolitan Museum, encircled by his paintings and drinking champagne with his admirers. Which included his family: his father bursting with pride, his moth-er fluttering excitedly, Maeve and Alex awed by the fame of their little brother. Oh, there must be genius in him, some-thing unique, that other, more commonplace people could not see. He knew it must be so. He remembered that wound in his palm: *stigmata.*

He was brought sharply back to the present by his mother, who was declaring irritably that it was time to go. They took a taxi, although the restaurant was very near, because Celia pre-ferred to be driven home. Entering their apartment, turning on the lights and throwing her scarf over the arm of a Louis XIV chair, she favoured her family with a smile and cried, "Now, didn't we all have an FNO?" Fifth Avenue shorthand for "fine night out".

1995

A flurry of nuns swept him along the too-bright corridor. He tried to escape, pushing past their stiff robes; at one point, alarmingly, a breast brushed his arm – a nun's breast, warm as any woman's beneath that dowdy habit! But why should he be surprised? Had he thought nuns were made of vapour from the wimple down? Confused, and for some reason slightly angry, he stumbled next into a grey-suited businessman. "Where's the bar?" he blurted.

"Just behind you," the man answered easily. Gabriel turned around, and indeed there it was, dim as a brothel like most American bars, even in this glaring airport terminal, with *Budweiser* and *Coors* scrolled in neon above the bottles of beer and whiskey. "Thanks," he mumbled and hurried in, anxious for a fortifying drink before his flight.

He ordered a double Jack Daniels and said goodbye to New York. Something trembled through him, composed of regret and dismay, but also possibility, the promise of a new life.

• • •

The air hostess was distributing Irish newspapers. He read them intently. Whole pages devoted to poets and novelists! What a country! And the art exhibitions actually seemed sane, as opposed to New York, where the newest star was a man who displayed his own vomit behind glass panels, accompanied by posters which read: YOU ARE EFFLUVIUM and FOOD FOR THOUGHT.

I will show them, he promised himself; *I will not give up.* New York had tried to humiliate him, but he was not broken.

He realised that once again he was angry, in the way he was always angry, a wild fury alloyed with a wild grief. He was a real artist, but they had driven him away.

He clenched his fists. The New York art scene had grown impossible. And Ireland's beauty would inspire him to new heights of achievement, while the raw American landscape had done nothing for him.

As the plane took off, he gazed out at that diminishing land-scape and at the harsh North American sky. *Yes,* he thought fiercely, *I am through with you, America. Through with your entrepreneurial mean-spiritedness, your disgusting pop culture, your refusal to honour genius, your general philistinism: I am beginning a new life.*

Calm down. He had registered that a woman seated across the aisle was staring at him. He must look weird, trembling, grinding his teeth. Maybe she thought he was terrified of flying? If she tried to comfort him, he would give her a piece of his mind. He forced himself to throw her a smile. Immediately she relaxed and smiled timidly back. Ah, he observed wearily, she is happy now. It was all too easy for him to bestow happi-ness on others, since he was so *talented,* so *handsome,* so *charm-ing.* All he had to do was smile, and the ladies trembled, the people rejoiced. He half-believed he deserved their homage and half-believed they deserved his contempt. After all, they must be contemptible, if they couldn't see through him.

The air hostess roused him for breakfast. As always, approaching Ireland, he marvelled that the sky was different here, the clouds radiant, the distances brocaded with gold. He was thirty-five and had been coming to Ireland all his life, but with each return his love of it struck him full in the heart. *Home,* he thought now, clenching his fists again.

Chapter 1

TONY WAS IN Seamus O'Sullivan's food shop, buying smoked mackerel for his supper, when he saw her. He did not know why she caught his attention; she was nothing special really, a tired-looking woman, nearly old enough, he guessed, to be his mother.

It seemed to have something to do with a movement of her hand. She was regarding the vegetables when she lifted her hand and pushed back the hair at her temple. It was unremarkable hair, fine, blondish, falling to her shoulders. But something in her way of pushing it back – a weariness about it, an impatience and a weariness – convinced him that she was deeply intelligent, and deeply unhappy. And, for some reason, that gesture, the lifting of her arm, the ungentle pushing back of the hair above her ear, for some reason it pierced him to the quick. He felt in his arm the weight of her arm drawn up; he felt in his own hand the weary, rather unfeminine motion of her hand, pushing back the stubborn hair which had moved forward to spray into her eyes. He felt these things; he felt her in himself. Clutching a packet of Union Hall smoked mackerel, he stared at her, a forty-year-old woman, dressed in jeans and a not-too-clean yellow jumper, with fairish hair drooping around a tired face. He realised that she would haunt him now, and he had no idea why.

He sidled up to the vegetables and pretended to consider them: boulders of turnip, new potatoes (for this was spring), cabbages whose outer fronds were as opulently ruffled as the sleeves of Restoration courtiers, leeks with their flat eucalyptus-like tops, lustrous Euro-aubergines, even Euro-ginger and Euro-garlic, since O'Sullivan's had become a sophisticated shop, much frequented by the Continental tourists.

Sensing his presence, the woman glanced at him. Tony almost never registered the colour of people's eyes, but he noticed immediately that hers were a light yellow-gold, like a honeycomb. In fact they were almost the same colour as her hair. She smiled vaguely, then turned back to the onions, some of which she was putting into a rush basket at her feet.

He continued to observe her surreptitiously while pretending to contemplate the courgettes, and once again she made that gesture, pushing back her hair with the flat of her hand, rather roughly. He had known women, vain women, to caress their hair, to curl strands of it round their finger; he had known nervous women to touch their hair incessantly – for reassurance, he supposed. But this thoughtless, impatient gesture by an unknown woman was new to him and unaccountably moving. It made the breath catch in his throat, as though he were gazing at something beautiful or else heartbreaking.

Impulsively he said, "I think I know you. Don't I know you?"

She looked at him with, he thought, annoyance. But she was English; he knew that she was English the moment she spoke, and like all polite Englishwomen she was adept at concealing her annoyance almost immediately behind a polite, rebuffing smile. "No, I shouldn't think so. No, I am afraid you are mistaken. Won't you excuse me?" She hoisted up her rush basket – heavy with onions, bunches of herbs, eggs, apples, a cheese – and carried it past him to the till.

He moved dispiritedly through the shop, buying a lemon for his mackerel, a container of Greek yoghurt, some toothpaste. He didn't need the toothpaste, but wanted to remain close to the woman for as long as possible. Her rebuff had not daunted him, which was surprising, for he was usually quite diffident. He even considered abandoning his provisions and following her out of the shop, but Seamus O'Sullivan had seen him and was beckoning him up to the counter.

"Hello, Tony," cried Seamus in his bluff way. "How's the old painting going?"

"Grand," answered Tony distractedly. "I've got another exhibition coming up next month, in Ballybracken. That woman who just left the shop – who is she?"

"Why, that would be Fleur," Seamus said promptly, putting Tony's meagre purchases into a plastic carrier bag, "Fleur York. She lives near to yourself, in that old farmhouse used belong to Ginger Kiely before he collapsed one morning toasting a cake of brown soda for his breakfast and had to be taken by ambulance to Bantry Hospital, and now he's living with the sister above in Cork for he's no longer able to do for himself. It's Ginger's house she'd be living in. Fleur York is her name, and she'd be a painter or a sculptor, like yourself." He placed the bag in Tony's hands. "That'll be twelve pounds, so."

"*Twelve?* For a lemon—"

"You're forgetting all those *Irish Timeses* and that bottle of wine you hadn't the change for yesterday."

"Oh, right. Sorry." Tony rummaged in his pockets; at the same time he caught his reflection in the mirror behind Seamus' head. He was dismayed by what he saw, by his too-long messy black hair, forlorn brown spaniel eyes, crooked nose. Although he was twenty-five and already a fairly successful painter, this adolescent shyness still lingered in him, a self-consciousness about things like big feet, lumpy Adam's apple, thinness, general clumsiness.

Emerging from the shop, he saw the woman again, opening the door of a small yellow car. She was tallish and lean, like himself. She got in and drove away in the direction of his own house. He realised, with alarm, that his eyes were full of tears.

• • •

Tony Daly had been born in America, but because his father was an academic – a psychology professor of some renown – he had always travelled, much like the children of diplomats or soldiers. As far back as Tony could remember, universities were for ever enticing his father away, so that the Daly family were for ever voyaging, to another state within the States or to another country, to yet another drowsy university town or impersonal city. Tony had lived in New York and Wisconsin, in Mexico City and Paris, in Florence and Kyoto. But when the time came for him to attend university himself, he chose art college and Dublin; and afterwards West Cork, to paint and to live.

His house (actually the house of an absent friend, now in London, to whom Tony posted one hundred pounds each month) was in a deep valley. Its garden was lush, with lichen-mottled trees, a profusion of flowers and a mossy pool. Ivy shawled the house itself, and scarlet fuchsia swarmed around the old cow byre. Across the road, beyond Farmer Coughlan's fields, the distances glowed, as though the ocean were very near. This was an illusion; it was actually a number of miles away. But that low sky which seemed to flower with light-quicksilver clouds and splashes of gold suggested the presence of the sea, as did the mountains themselves, clothed with vapour each morning, exhaling a marine fluorescence in the afternoon. At dawn, when Tony opened his door upon a golden haze beneath the trees, grass glinting with dew, vivid hedges, Farmer Cough-lan's fields and, finally, the mountains, it was as though all perspectives were foreshortened here. Everything was close – garden, fields, sky, sea – everything within his compass. He could extend his arm and embrace the world, or so it seemed. At dawn there was the wooden-flute sound of the cuckoo; often he would see rabbits, more rarely a badger. Because he left crumbs for the birds, they had made his garden their sanctuary and were nearly unafraid of him. A girl had broken his heart in Dublin, and so he thought he would be content to live alone now, to love the beauty of this place as he would have loved a woman, to paint, to read, to take long walks, collecting wild-flowers and white heather. But then his peace was disturbed,

absurdly, by an unremarkable woman – a middle-aged woman!
– in a shop.

•••

When he arrived home that evening, after seeing Fleur York for
the first time, Tony was restive, unable to work or read. Presently he made his supper: the salty mackerel, a green salad, some
local cheese and brown bread, with one glass of white wine,
then one of red.

He was remembering the first time he had come to this valley, Glenfern. It was winter, and on his first night the moon
was full. He had walked along the chill road, and the trees had
been black and hard as iron in the moonlight. A silver smoke
had seemed to hover just above the earth, and each field and
slope had been filmed with this bleak radiance. It was winter,
but he had known, walking through his own new cold valley,
that spring was coming, that soon the yellow gorse would
flare along these fields and that the fuchsia would blossom.
He had stopped to touch a stone wall crusted over with brack-
en, and, feeling the stalks like some coarse fabric on his fingers, he had sensed the living past in this country, had *felt* the
human mysteries which were housed here. The stone wall he
was touching, with its web of flowering things even in winter,
seemed to emerge from the earth itself, and he realised that
anyone living here could summon forth ghosts if they tried,
since ghosts were all around: Bronze Age and Iron Age, pre-
Celt and Celt, rebellion and famine, joy and lamentation. It
was in the land; it was alive. He had come to Glenfern with a
broken heart, but on that first night he had finally believed
his heart would mend.

Now, on an evening in spring, he had lost his repose. He poured himself a whiskey and glowered out at the lawn. It was not yet dark. Suddenly he put down his glass, strode out into the herb garden and began to gather up parsley, marjoram, mint, rosemary. The bruised herbs spilled their smells into the air, a cow lowed in the distance, a fly blundered against his face. He bunched the leaves – frilled, flat, bristling, spiny – into a bouquet, stood up and loped off in the direction of Ginger Kiely's farmhouse.

"I have brought you some herbs," he announced, proffering the bouquet.

She stood on the threshold, pushing the hair away from her forehead. She did not smile. With a kind of terror he wondered if they would stand like that interminably, he extending his ragged bundle of herbs and grinning like an idiot, she gazing impassively at him, neither speaking nor inviting him in.

Presently she said, "You grow herbs?"

"No. My friend Hugh, whose house I am living in, he does – did. He's in London now." Tony paused, feeling more and more foolish. "Hugh is an anthropologist," he finished weakly.

"I know. I have met him. I suppose you had better come in, before the midges devour you."

It was true. Although the evening was beautiful, cool and ripening towards dusk, a thousand midges had settled in his hair and were nibbling at his ears. He had been wanting to shake his head in order to scatter them but had refrained for fear of looking doglike. Now, gratefully, he followed her into her big kitchen. There was a large pot on the cooker, issuing savoury smells.

Without offering him a chair or a drink – in fact without speaking at all – she proceeded to wash and dry the herbs, and then to chop them up with a professional-looking knife and throw them into the pot.

"Soup," she explained tersely. "It will be ready soon."

He did not tell her that he had already eaten. She said, "Do make us a drink, if you don't mind. There is gin in the cupboard and lemons and tonic in the fridge."

Pouring generous measures into two of her thick glasses, he marvelled at her peculiar balance of rudeness and civility. None of the customary courtesies had been exchanged; he presumed she knew neither his name nor anything about him. She had been dismayingly brusque, peremptory to the point of surliness, but, on the other hand, she was obviously expecting him to drink and dine with her and had used his herbs in her cooking, which he supposed was an oblique expression of thanks.

He passed her a drink and settled with his own at the broad wooden table. Pretending to examine a book which was there – a biography of Jackson Pollock – he covertly observed her. She had changed from her jeans and yellow jumper into a loose, short-sleeved white dress, and he thought that she had washed her hair. It was not as thin and lustreless as he had first thought. In fact, it billowed slightly, perhaps because it was newly washed, and in the light of her lamps it was a deep gold, though he could also detect threads of grey. Her face, too, looked prettier now. She was not a beautiful woman, but her wide yellowy eyes, her somewhat sad expression, her slightly burnished complexion, were all attractive to him: there was a suggestion of the pre-Raphaelite about her. She moved efficiently through the room, throwing salt into the soup, putting a blue cheese on a plate with some home-made-looking bread, opening a bottle of wine. She did not ask for his help, nor did he offer it. He only drank his gin and looked at her, while night fell and the air outside grew warm with birdsong.

He had known the soup would be delicious, and it was. They drank it in silence, but when she served the wine, along with the cheese and her own bread, they both relaxed and began to talk.

She asked, "How long have you lived here?"

When he replied his jaw felt wooden, a sign that he was a bit drunk. Making an especial effort to enunciate clearly, he told her he had arrived in Ballycurry two years ago. Within that period he had managed to achieve some modest success as a painter, not only locally but nationally, with a first exhibition in Dublin and good notices in the press. Indeed, a cross-border, non-sectarian women's organisation had recently purchased one of his landscapes, a dove flying over a bog pool, to use for their poster celebrating the IRA ceasefire, which had started the year before.

In exchange for this information, Fleur told him that she had bought Ginger Kiely's house two and a half years ago but, until recently, had occupied it only now and again, living mainly in London. She did not explain why her life had changed, why now, presumably, she had settled in Glenfern.

"Incidentally," she said, "I am Fleur York, and like you I am a painter. Only for my work I use my maiden name."

"You're married?" he queried gauchely; then swallowed hard, feeling once again like a fool.

She gave him a peculiar look, half-amused, half-wintry.

"Divorced. My working name is Penhalligan. A Cornish name; my people are from Cornwall."

He felt his face redden. "Fleur Penhalligan! I had no idea. You're, well, you're a famous—"

"Never mind. Please have more cheese. You haven't told me your own name, Strange Visitor."

"Maybe I shouldn't tell you. Maybe I should remain Strange Visitor, who comes to your door bearing gifts of marjoram and rosemary."

She smiled. He observed that when she smiled, one realised how sad her expression was most of the time. The smile transformed her into a young woman.

As though reading his mind, she said gently, "I am quite old, you know, forty-two. If you feel inclined to call on people and give them presents from your garden, perhaps you ought to choose someone closer to your own age?"

Again he blushed, maddeningly. If he turned scarlet each time she flustered him, he'd never convince her that he was mature enough to be her friend.

"I don't care about age," he declared hotly. "I was an only child, so very early on I got used to being around people older than myself. When I was small, my parents and their colleagues interested me far more than other children. I never felt close to people my own age. . ."

He paused. The strong gin and all the wine he had drunk were making him reckless. "Especially women. Girls in their twenties are so self-absorbed. And they're either terrified of close relationships, or else they want to engulf you." He hesitated again before plunging onwards. "What I'm saying is, I felt drawn to you in the shop today, and I would like to get to know you better. We *are* neighbours, after all."

He looked cautiously at her, but she didn't seem offended. She was gazing quietly at him, the fingers of her right hand playing with the crumbs on her plate. "My name is Tony Daly," he concluded in a faint voice. He was feeling exhausted.

After a while she said thoughtfully, "Tomorrow I am going to London, but I shall be back next week. If you would like, you may come to dinner then. I'll make a proper meal, not just soup and bits of things. You may come then. Perhaps Thursday."

The joy he felt was pure, primordial. All his life he had feared loss. As a child he'd had a recurring nightmare, in which he would be alone in the streets of a bustling city, crying out to indifferent people. A kindly man or woman would stop to help him, but he had lost the address he was looking for; he was lost, utterly, so that even the kindest of citizens was helpless to succour him. Yet now in this old-fashioned kitchen, he had been given an inkling of grace. He smiled. "Yes," he said, "that would be very nice."

When he got up to leave, his stomach felt curiously distended; then he realised he'd eaten two meals that evening. She walked him to the door. He wanted desperately to kiss her, to take her in his arms, if only briefly, to feel the cool stuff of her dress on his hands and to kiss that sad mouth.

She extended her cheek and he brushed his lips against it, catching the camomile smell of her hair.

She said, "You are a peculiar and pleasant young man. I am glad to have met you. And thank you for the herbs, Strange Visitor."

• • •

He'd been terrified of doctors as a little boy. When he'd had to go for those tiresome obligatory visits to which children are eternally subjected, the whole day would be plunged in gloom. Had he been afraid that the doctor would pronounce him terminally ill or that he would be torn from his parents and thrown into some murky hospital? He could not remember, now, the exact reason for his dread, only its nature. He had tried to bargain with God for a measure of grace on those doctor-visit days. He would be extremely courteous to his mother, father, teddy bear, during those hours before he was to travel to surgery or clinic, as though, if he were only a good enough boy, the mysterious forces that governed his life might have mercy on him.

Now, walking home in the darkness, Tony understood that this was how he had always lived, convinced on some level that he was undeserving, appealing, through good behaviour, for a better portion, bargaining for love. Only, now, tonight, this woman had not minded his silliness, drunkenness, social awkwardness. As he strode along the road, he began to sing, inanely:

> *South of the Border*
> *Down West Cork Way;*
> *That's where I met her*
> *When the stars came out to play…*

Chapter 2

GABRIEL'S GRANDMOTHER HAD bequeathed him a house in Glenfern townland. It was not the house in which she herself had lived. *That* monstrosity, a turreted Victorian pile close to Castletownshend, had gone to Maeve, Granny's favourite. The Glenfern house was a legacy from Gabriel's grandfather's family, and it was much smaller than Maeve's grim palace, but Gabriel was pleased with it and with the valley. He had first seen Glenfern in autumn, when the low mountains were bronze, russet and purple, like an old Irish tweed coat, and the hedges were a tapestry of bracken, jagged gorse and hard red haws.

That was only a reconnaissance mission, and he'd left before winter's onslaught, before the cold and rain, before the long nights and grey mornings, the muddied gardens, the 'flus and chilblains. But he knew about the Irish winters, and he knew he wouldn't mind them. He liked grey weather, and he liked the old grey house with its blackened stove, trestle tables and big guest bedroom which could serve as a studio.

West Cork would welcome him. It had become a mecca for artists, this remote region in the extreme south-west of the westernmost island of Europe. It was burgeoning with small art galleries and studios, and the population was growing more and more international and bohemian. He would recreate himself here and prosper.

● ● ●

Why did Gabriel Phillips leave New York for good in the spring of 1995 to settle in Glenfern, Ballycurry, County Cork, Ireland? One might hazard that his decision had something to do with the IRA ceasefire, declared twelve months before; only Gabriel didn't care about the North. His mother's genteel Church of Ireland family had always regarded Northern Ireland as distant and uncouth, and its Troubles as faintly embarrassing. As for Gabriel himself, he had never been interested in politics, except when they encroached on the art world.

No, his reasons for coming to Ireland were mainly personal, to do with a woman.

He had met Ardyth at the movies. He had always loved movies, especially those old Hollywood films full of glamorous girls with clouds of hair, and tough guys smouldering beneath fedoras.

The night he met her was like an old film: a rainy night, people hurrying along the avenue, their umbrellas glistening under the street lamps. Since he hadn't brought an umbrella, Gabriel was waiting in the foyer of the cinema for the rain to ease. A young woman was standing there also.

"I might take a taxi," she said suddenly. "I might just give in and take a taxi, even though it's so expensive."

She was very pretty, with short auburn hair and large green eyes which drooped at their outer corners, giving her a slightly wistful expression.

They stared at each other. Gabriel said, "We could split the cost. Where do you live?" He felt he was in a movie.

"Uptown." She said the word slowly, like a plum, or as though she were in a movie.

"I'm afraid I live downtown, in SoHo."

She smiled. "That's okay. Downtown is okay."

• • •

Ardyth was a model. Her short hair and pert face with big downswerving eyes were fetching in a *gamine* way, although she was neither tall nor beautiful enough to make it as a high-powered supermodel.

But she didn't mind. She worked: that was the point, in a city full of aspirants. She worked mostly for catalogues, occasionally for magazines, and had appeared on a few music videos and television commercials. Her income was respectable, but she was far from well-off by Gabriel's standards.

That first night, sauntering into his loft, she had immediately taken off her blouse, which had got wet despite the taxi. He had loved how, without speaking, she idly undid the buttons and threw the thing over a chair (she was wearing no bra) while he poured them each a glass of wine. Next, he'd admired how she took the glass from his hand, smiling politely, as though she were not standing half-naked in a stranger's room.

Rain spattered against the windows. They touched glasses. Again he had the eerie but not unpleasant sensation of being in a film. Boy and girl in airy loft, standing face to face while the dark windows shudder with rain, girl audaciously half-naked, boy accepting the challenge. The director was telling them that the time had come for some Bogart-style repartee.

"Do you always take your clothes off when you enter a room?"

"Only when I'm wet."

Gabriel considered that this reply might have pitched beyond witty *film noir* dialogue into mere vulgarity, but he liked it all the same.

She said, "So, you're a painter?"

"To the dismay of my family."

He brought her into his studio, where she looked solemnly at the paintings and he looked at her small breasts and smooth arms which were subtly glossed with an auburn down.

"I don't know much about painting," she declared finally, swallowing the last of her wine and extending the glass for more.

"With that statement you have dismissed four years of dedication and back-breaking labour."

"You don't look like a man with a broken back."

They had returned to the kitchen. She put her glass down on the counter, grasped his wrists and moved his hands on to her breasts, which were still damp from the rain, the nipples hard as pellets against his palm. After that there was no more talk, as though the director, whoever he (or she) was, had decreed it should be so.

•••

A few months later, Ardyth told him, with her customary thoughtless cruelty, that when they'd first met she had presumed he was a *successful* painter, because, after all, he was living in SoHo, among the fashionable artists.

Her words wounded him more than he let her see, since they were true: he occupied a loft in SoHo not because he was a recognised painter on whom the arts foundations had lavished support, but simply because he was rich enough to live where he pleased. And if he had unconsciously believed that a SoHo address would enhance his fortunes, deepen his gift, enable him to soar, he had been wrong; the address had no magical properties. And his artist neighbours, most of whom had settled in SoHo when it was merely a dour industrial area – not at all the elegant quarter it had since become – and had weathered rough times before attaining success, were vaguely polite, but did not champion him.

He loved SoHo. He loved the bohemian air of it, he loved the presence of the river – a pearl light in the sky – he loved the old iron warehouses, the redolent spice markets, the offbeat bars, the magical feeling of an urban area where utterly different worlds mingle, in this instance the grimly industrial and ebulliently artistic. He didn't mind the commercialisation and hype; he barely noticed those things. He only wanted to paint. He presumed that some of his neighbours resented him because they were living in lofts under special dispensations for artists, while he'd breezed in solely on the strength of his father's money. But he had thought he could woo them to his side.

He visited them and talked passionately about painting, about Delaunay, who was his hero, about how he himself was working on canvases composed entirely of light and colour, like the paintings of Delaunay. His neighbours listened politely, their paint-smudged hands clasped. But they did not call to see him, and he was given no opportunities to exhibit, although a few of his mother's friends bought paintings from him, and a woman reporter he'd met at a party came up one day to see his work and praised it afterwards in a local arts magazine.

Lately he was doing something different: painting SoHo itself, those streets of disconcertingly ornate warehouses with their metal awnings, and thickets of fire escapes. He was pleased with these canvases, which seemed to depict cities and forests at the same time, and even Ardyth said that they were "cool".

One morning he struck her. She had been provoking him, spiralling him into a primitive and familiar place. It was curious how fast it happened, that plunge into darkness. All of a sudden he was no longer the confident painter, but a small boy sweating with fear in his mother's bedroom. His mother was slowly taking off her jewellery, carefully unfastening the clasps of her bracelets, tilting her head to undo a pearl necklace. She was not looking at him, only down at her dressing table where the jewels, glittering, were looped and strewn. He stared at her exposed white nape.

"You are a bad boy," she was saying softly. "Your father will have to punish you. I cannot protect you the whole time, Gabriel."

"But I didn't do it," he answered in a voice thick with terror. "It was Maeve. She thought it would be funny to put sugar in Simone's salt cellar—"

"Hush. It is most ungentlemanly to betray your sister. If you speak like that to your father, he will only hurt you more. You must take your punishment like a man." Finally she turned to him, smiling sadly.

"Why *won't* you protect me?" he asked wildly. "I massaged your feet this morning, the way you like me to. . ." He thought, but did not say, *even though it embarrasses me to do those things, to massage your feet, to choose your dresses for you, comb your hair. . .*

"You know how your father is," she said sternly. "You know he'll not listen to me when he's angry." She gave him another pitying smile. "Sometimes I think he's a bit jealous of you, my pet, since you and I get along so well. Anyway, you will have to go out there and face the music. I *cannot* protect you. Off you go."

The beating had been severe.

He had hated her, and his father as well, but, most of all, he'd hated himself, because they made him feel that he was nothing. And when Ardyth taunted him he was again nothing, spiralling down and down, and in a familiar sweat of rage and pain he struck her and was surprised when it felt good, when the crack of his palm against her cheek was exhilarating. It was as though all those years of a child's inarticulate terror, all those humiliations, all that loneliness, were expunged, at last, by this final abandonment of caution.

And after he'd begun, it was easier to keep on going, easier to strike again than to stop. And when her green eyes blazed with anger, when she cried, "You *bastard*," and made to strike back, then it was real sport, with lamps toppling, clothes tearing, rage and sex all mixed up, so that soon he didn't know – or care – which was which.

Ardyth liked it, that much was clear. In the middle of it all, she began to breathe heavily, to reach for him with avid fingers. They were on the floor; he had pushed her dressing gown up above her waist and was parting her legs with his knees. She clutched at his shirt; suddenly he drew his arm back and gave her another crack across the cheek. They stared at each other. He realised that striking her about the face was somehow more intimate, and a greater violation, than the rape he had been intending to commit; that to see her face reddened like this from the blows he had dealt it was a bigger turn-on than the spread legs, and naked sex between his knees. She seized him by the hair. *"Do it again,"* she commanded through clenched teeth. *"Do it again."*

For days afterwards they were both contrite, looking at each other with abashed, nearly frightened eyes. Ardyth was so tactful it was painful to him, as though someone close to him had died and she knew that he was grieving. He was suddenly aware of how childlike she was, with her gawky arms and street-urchin face. The whole loft seemed plunged into mourning. They had realised that they were both damaged. They were in mourning for themselves. Every night they made love, tenderly, desperately, and often she cried herself to sleep beside him on the pillow.

He tried to comfort her. He was ashamed of the things he had done to her and afraid of the dark place in himself out of which the violence had risen, like a serpent swerving up from a bedful of snakes. He had been like someone possessed, but Ardyth had also been possessed, and what he feared most was the animal that they had both created, the flailing hissing thing to which they had given birth on that day. And once born, could it die, or would it appear again and rend them?

He thought he should ask Ardyth more about her own past, but some obscure fear of what she might reveal restrained him. So, instead, he tried to comfort her with feeble gestures, half apologies, until, one day, she put her fingers against his mouth and said, "Let it go, Gabriel."

A late morning about two months afterwards, he was painting very well, better than ever. Sunlight was clouding in through the studio window, and in this mist of light his colours sang: lapis lazuli; smoky violet; chill blue; blood-bright garnet. He felt *real*.

Ardyth had walked up behind him. He thought she must be admiring his canvas and the intensity of his concentration, but what she said was, "You look so silly, Gabriel, the way you keep staring at that thing with your eyes half-closed, like you think you're in some garret in Paris or something. Like an actor *pretending* to be an artist."

He whirled round and smashed her one. She let out a wail of fear which might have restrained him if she had not fallen against his work table, scattering brushes, palette and knives all over the floor, and infuriating him so much that he lost control utterly and really thought he might kill her. Bad enough that she had laughed at him, but now it would be hours before he could reassemble his materials and try to work again, with her insults still beating in his ears. He knew she had done it all deliberately, taunting him in the same way as his father, sabotaging his work out of jealousy, trying to trample on his self-confidence. Even upsetting his work table had probably been deliberate.

"Not my face, not my face!" she screamed, and despite his paroxysm of rage he considered that this was a reasonable entreaty, since she wouldn't be able to work with black eyes or a broken nose. So he limited himself to her body, giving her rabbit and kidney punches, just as his father had given him, because the bruises wouldn't show. She might be in pain, gliding down the catwalk, but no one would detect it, and Gabriel admired his generosity in the face of her abuse of him.

But he had gone too far, after all. When he was spent, she did not move, only lay there breathing strangely, her face white. Suddenly terrified, he did all he could to revive her, splashing cold water on her face, crying out her name. Finally, full of fury and remorse, he called for an ambulance.

• • •

A month later, he was in his father's sombre study, to which he had been summoned, as though he were merely another client. His father was behind his vast desk, hands clasped, face pallid with anger. Gabriel kept getting up to walk around; he knew this annoyed Matthew, which was probably why he was doing it.

"This has been awkward for us all, Gabriel," his father was saying, in a voice bladed with rage. "Very, very awkward. Your mother is distraught, and it has been hard for your sisters to bear up under this disgrace to which you have so thoughtlessly subjected us."

Gabriel stood by the window, looking out at Central Park. "At least I didn't kill her. And your belief that *you* are the wounded party in all this strikes me as pretty ironic, with that poor bitch still in bed recovering from internal injuries and me the villain of the piece."

"It is in extremely poor taste for you to speak so flippantly. It was I rescued you from scandal, from prison, from having your name splashed all over the media."

"Sharper than a serpent's tooth." Gabriel laughed harshly, then returned to his chair and gazed blandly at his father, whose discomfiture he was savouring. It was as though his fall from grace had finally released him from Matthew's spell. He didn't give a flying fuck any more what this pompous old hypocrite might think of him. Anyway, from whom had Gabriel learnt how to beat the living daylights out of somebody, a detail his self-righteous prick of a so-called father was conveniently choosing to ignore? As for his mother, she had betrayed him time and again with her unseemly coquetry and her cowardice, and his sisters had become boring women of means, with "good" marriages, and ostentatious mink coats. They could all go to hell, as far as he was concerned.

"You are fortunate that the poor girl will recover and that we were able to buy her silence. You are not intending to see her again, are you?"

He had tried, walking tentatively into her hospital room (he'd been astounded when the nurse at Registration, consulting a column of names, told him that he was permitted to visit her). She had looked small and lost against the white pillows, her eyes enormous and green as bottle glass. At first she had shrunk back, with a rabbit-caught-in-the-headlamps expression, but then, "I'll get you," she had cried, "I'll *kill* you for this, you sick bastard. My lawyer says—"

"All right, Ardyth. Let's just say we weren't good for each other." He'd left his peace offering of a dozen red roses on the bed and walked out, for ever.

"You will have to leave New York," his father was telling him. "Your continuing presence here would inflict too much humiliation on your mother. You will have to go as far away as possible. South-east Asia, perhaps, where they don't mind your kind of person. My contacts in Bangkok–"

"I am not going to Bangkok, Father. I'm going home, to Ireland."

Matthew stared bleakly at him, worrying a pencil in his fingers. Presently he said slowly, "All right, Gabriel. You have your grandmother's house. You might go there. I will give you a generous allowance, as long as you don't return." He paused. "There is the problem of Maeve's summer place, in Castletownshend."

"You are saying I must never call on her? Don't worry, Father. Maeve is as vain a little cunt as I've ever met. I have no desire to speak to her again. What's the matter, Dad? I saw you blanch a bit there. Don't like my diction? Well, we all know what an upstanding citizen *you* are. *You'd* never utter an obscenity, would you, you philandering child-beater." He tilted forward in his chair. There was a rage coursing through him strong as dark wine. So *this* was the source, *this* the wound in the heart, the origin of the emptiness which sometimes afflicted him like a wasting sickness, *this* the torn place in his spirit, which would never be mended. Poor Ardyth, poor stand-in! His mouth rich with bile, he said softly, "Don't worry, Dad. You and Mother will never see me again. You're quit of me, and I of you, thank God, although I wish it had happened at my birth."

He got up and moved towards the door. From the corner of his eye, he saw Matthew extend a hand, and he paused, still half-looking back, his fingers on the handle of the half-open door. But his father neither rose nor spoke. So Gabriel walked out.

Chapter 3

TONY WAS USED to a different sun, brighter, stronger. Conjuring up America, he remembered cars surging along the highways, their windows glinting like knife-blades in the summer sun. (Even when people tried to live off the main drag, there was still the throb of traffic beyond the trees, unless they burrowed further and further in, as though in flight.) He remembered cloudless skies bleached with a dry midday light and evenings when the sky turned bronze, the air cooled subtly, and there was a sudden smell of exhausted earth.

In damp Ireland the sun was diffuse, blurred, mysterious. On clear evenings in Glenfern, the fields themselves were charged with light, a golden glow, as though they had soaked up all that day's sun and would exhale it, now, back into the sky, which was never still. Clouds billowed across it, a slow procession, while Tony stared and stared, wondering would he ever be able to paint such a wild light?

He was working in sheer washes of colour, experimenting. One painting, of the sky at daybreak – at that precise moment when the cuckoo's cry trembles the silence – had actually frightened him. He didn't know where it had come from, but it seemed to contain the sound of the cuckoo. He had turned its face to the wall, refusing to look at it.

Thursday, when he was to visit Fleur again, he felt overcome with anxiety. After their first meeting he had been jubilant, as though he had broken through the membrane of his awkwardness and come into a warm place where his shyness would be banished for ever. But now that he was to see her once more, it was as though their first encounter had been a dream. He was timid again as he walked along the road in the inevitable cloud of evening midges, carrying two bottles of Spanish red in a paper bag.

When he arrived he was dismayed to see that she was not alone. Another woman was standing with her in the garden, a "crusty", Tony thought sullenly. Crusties were New Age hippies who had taken refuge in West Cork from the over-industrialised cities of England and the Continent. Observing them over their glasses of beer or cider in MacCarthy's pub, he had been intrigued by them. After all, they had renounced former lives to work here as organic farmers or carpenters, and Tony had wanted to hear their stories. But, now, observing this woman with her Rastafarian hairdo and ragamuffin clothes, talking intently to *his* new friend, he immediately decided that they were all feckless, arrogant and smelly.

"Hello, Strange Visitor." Fleur smiled, extending a hand, which he could not take because of the wine bottles. The crusty woman stared speculatively at him. She was about his own age, with minute eyes in a whey-coloured face. If she stayed to dinner, he would die, or else excuse himself and leave early.

Fleur introduced her as "Inge, who lives along the Bally-bracken road". Then, "I'll be off now," said this Inge in a German accent, and Tony was so grateful, he could have kissed her. *She's actually quite pleasant*, he thought, *quite a nice woman, after all.*

They went into the kitchen, where, once again, he settled at the table (this time laid with yellow plates on a green cloth) while she prepared the meal. "You mustn't help me," she said. "I can't bear to have people underfoot while I'm cooking. Just pour yourself a Tio Pepe and talk to me."

She was wearing a sleeveless pink dress with a pattern of small blue flowers, a necklace of blue stones and blue *espadrilles*. Her arms and bare legs had turned brown, and the hair eddying over her shoulders was subtly paler. In the lamplight her face, too, had changed, was warmer, rosier, the eyes topaz-bright.

"You have been in the sun," he observed, and at the precise moment of uttering that phrase, another, soundless voice in his head whispered, *I love you.*

"I wasn't lolling on a beach. It's just that London was so hot this year, I got all brown simply by walking."

"Did you enjoy London?"

She placed, in the centre of the table, a plate of avocado-crescents and bright tomatoes dressed with oil and basil. "No. I was there to meet my . . . ex-husband. We had business to discuss. It was boring and sordid, actually."

He had felt from the first that she was sad. And he liked how she talked to him about it: tersely, without affectation. During their previous meeting, he had thought her rather rude, but now he realised that she was simply – sometimes uncomfortably – forthright. He said, "It must be awful, when people who used to love each other are reduced to talking only about money, as though they had never been anything but business partners."

Putting some of the avocado and tomato on both their yellow plates and pouring wine into their glasses, she gave him one of her half-amused, half-wry looks. Presently, while they were eating, she said, "My ex-husband – whose name is Nicholas – is not a bad man, but he is naturally polygamous. And I am not. At one time I would have been ashamed to admit that. It would have seemed an uncool, middle-class attitude. But now I think it is merely a matter of temperament. I think I shall always regard love between a couple as something intimate, nearly holy. If they try to portion it out to others, the intimacy between them ceases to exist. At least this is how I have found things."

Trying to imagine Nicholas, Tony pictured a handsome man, defiant in his infidelities, regarding Fleur's distress at them as boringly bourgeois, admonishing her to loosen up. She would have tried, painting well into the night in her chill London studio, hearing, finally, his tread in the bedroom below, then descending reluctantly, to lie with dry, open eyes beside him while he slept.

"I believe in monogamy, too," he answered. "Of course, in my generation, we *have* to, whatever our temperament. Casual sex has become too dangerous."

Laughing softly, she got up, removing their plates. Presently she returned with fresh, warmed ones, and then with the next course. She had made a roast lamb, pink in the middle and scented with garlic, and roasted potatoes, and the first, tender asparagus of the season, with hollandaise sauce. He poured more wine.

She resumed, "I stopped loving Nicholas quite a while ago. He had damaged my love for him so repeatedly, and I was so exhausted, it finally just died. Curiously, it was he who was thrown into anguish at the prospect of the divorce. He hadn't thought anything was wrong with our marriage; he could never understand my loneliness. He believed that he loved me, and he insisted that the other women had never mattered. So when I applied for a divorce, he had a . . . I suppose one says a break-down, a nervous breakdown." She paused, putting a piece of lamb into her mouth. Tony did not speak.

After a moment she said, "It was horrible, and I felt – I still feel – so guilty. But I couldn't go back. That would have been cowardly, and no help to either of us. There was no trust, you see, or love. But even now, in London, he implored me . . ." Suddenly she put her knife and fork on the plate and stared down at it, her hands in her lap.

"Maybe you shouldn't talk about this. It's making you lose your appetite, and your dinner is so delicious."

She smiled and gamely took up the cutlery again. They ate in silence for a while, then she asked him about his own history, and he described his brilliant but daunting father, how it had been hard to live with a psychologist, since you always had the feeling that he was divining your private thoughts. He had been closer to his mother, a mild woman resigned to her position as faculty wife, adjusting easily to life in this country or that. He spoke about his love affair with the girl in Dublin, how she had abandoned him for another art student, an Anglo-Irish bore with many port wine pretensions but little talent. "Only now I am over her," he assured Fleur, gazing across the table at her haze of yellow hair, those serious eyes, "I am over her, at last."

"How old are you, Tony?" She had been clearing the table, once more insisting that he shouldn't help. Now she served them plates of strawberries covered with a cream that billowed beneath an ivory crust.

"Cornish clotted cream," she explained, "from my own village. It's one of the little things I miss, though I do love living here." Then, again, gently, "How old are you, Tony?"

"Nearly twenty-six," he mumbled, hoping that his cheeks weren't burning.

Abruptly she got up from the table and stood at the window, staring out at the night sky. He followed her. She turned around, her back against the wall, and said with dismay, "Oh, you are so young!"

"I'm *not*." And then he was kissing her, moulding his body to hers. At first she tried to wriggle away, but he had her pressed against the wall, and after a moment she was kissing him back, her hands in his hair. Through the light fabric of her dress he could feel her breasts, the delicate bones of her hips, her thighs, and he knew that she was feeling how excited he was, crushed against her. She began to move against him, while he kissed her mouth, her sun-warmed cheek, her ear. He pressed his thigh against her groin, feeling that they were defying the boundaries of their separate skins, had wound themselves into each other. Suddenly she gave a little cry and clutched at his sleeves. He looked at her. Her eyes were closed; strands of hair glinted across her cheeks and half-open mouth. She cried out again, then slumped and put her head on his shoulder.

He kept his arms around her. He didn't know if she was crying. Presently she looked up at him, and smiled. "Oh, God," she sighed. "Oh, God. If this is just the warm-up, I suppose we had better get to bed."

• • •

Her face was a woman's, but she had the body of a girl, smooth and slight, with narrow hips and breasts like flowers. He could not have foreseen it, but for some reason he was more confident than herself in her large bed. She was shy and hesitant, but for the first time in his sexual life he was self-assured and not urgent. He wanted to caress her slowly, to draw from her, again and again, those soft cries he had heard in the kitchen. After a while she was bolder and reached for him hungrily, and did things to him which made him also groan with pleasure.

They fell apart to sleep, only to stir awake and clasp each other again. Finally, at dawn, she burrowed into the pillow and slept deeply, but he remained open-eyed, not at all tired, staring out the window at the red-gold sky. For once he felt completely at peace.

He went softly down to the kitchen, brought their plates and glasses to the basin and washed up. Then he gathered up the green tablecloth and walked out into the garden to shake the crumbs from it – a meal for the birds. A silver web, each filament glinting with dew, clung to the hedge, trembling when a thrush took flight. He was naked, and the air was sweet as water against his skin.

He considered writing a message for her and leaving – perhaps she would like to be alone. But then he realised that this thought was a legacy from his days in America, where men and women seemed so stilted with each other, so afraid to expose their need for love. No, he would not skulk off home; he would go back up to her room and take her once again in his arms.

He slipped gingerly into bed, presuming she was still asleep, but she murmured, "I was afraid that you had gone away. I was afraid you were a dream."

"I am real," he said, "and I won't go away."

Chapter 4

GABRIEL WAS FOOTLOOSE, and glad of it. No family, no friends as yet, a farmhouse in Ireland, days and nights to himself, to paint, to listen to music, to reflect.

Looking back, he realised, with a kind of joyless satisfaction, that he had always been victimised. His mother, he could now see, had always been cold. Making love was distasteful to her, bearing children a painful nuisance. She had been Matthew's procuress, contemptuously arranging his liaisons with insignificant creatures, a secretary here, an ageing socialite there. She had castrated him with her indifference to the physical side of love and with her contempt for his appetites, and she had humiliated him further by transforming Gabriel into her accomplice, her lapdog, her little eunuch. His cheeks still burned when he remembered the nights in her bedroom, a fire glowing in the hearth, lighting the Rubens above her dressing table – all that cerise and pouting flesh – while she festooned him with her necklaces, caressing his head, her doll with doe

eyes. He had been her instrument; through him she had geld-
ed her husband, and therefore his father hated him.

If they had only loved him, protected him, he would be different now. On the other hand, that early ordeal was surely the
fire in which his genius had been tempered? He had little
doubt, now, that there was genius in him. There had been too
many signs and portents, too much suffering, for it not to be
so. Maeve and Alex had learnt early on to conform, but he had
always had a mutinous heart; there had always been something
different about him. That this "differentness" had marooned
him from more ordinary people, that it had sometimes inspired
envy and even dislike, this he took to be the price of his gift.
And if his parents' rejection of him were yet another price, he
was glad to pay it, glad to be banished from their world of opu-
lence and cruelty, in which no artist, let alone any sensitive spirit, could ever have survived intact. Ironically, their recognition
of him as someone unlike themselves had been a homage; their
forsaking of him a reverse kind of blessing.

Ardyth had victimised him, too. He understood this now.
She wasn't particularly intelligent, but there was a shrewdness
in her. She was adept at discerning where others were vulnerable, as when she had sidled up behind him in his studio and
taunted him for his concentration, as though he were just some
poseur. With her meagre, evanescent talent as a model, she must
have been galled by his greater gift, and so she had been determined to hurt him. In good conscience, he could no longer
blame himself for attacking her, since he had merely been
defending himself and his art. He knew that while he was fortunate to have been blessed with talent, he must not abuse the

gift or let others abuse it. The Muse did not brook neglect; an artist must do battle for his vision.

For the first week or so of his new life, he was reclusive, settling in, exploring the fields behind his house, rarely venturing further. A gentle old woman called Mrs O'Carroll "did" for him, coming every day to tidy and leaving a good meal on the cooker, an Irish stew or a roast chicken. But soon enough he decided that the time had come to attend exhibitions at the local galleries and to walk into Ballycurry for a drink at one or other of the brightly painted pubs. After all, he told himself, he *should* introduce himself to the local artists, some of whom were quite distinguished. Indeed, he had recently learnt from Mrs O'Carroll that the famous English painter, Fleur Penhalligan, actually lived along his very own road! Not that Mrs O'Carroll knew anything about painting, but she did know everything about everybody in Ballycurry, with her cleaning lady's access to their houses and her gossip's instinct for a juicy story.

Yet, as the spring days lengthened, he walked farther, into new fields, still mainly avoiding the village and the houses of his neighbours. He could only presume that the solace of nature, not humankind, was what his heart demanded now. As a child, visiting his granny in Castletownshend each summer, he had done this very thing, had walked for hours across fields, along back roads, through a mysterious cemetery full of lichened stones and ancient yews, then up to a famine burial ground and farther still, to a cluster of ruined cottages. His eyes had absorbed everything, streams coursing glassily over stones, the wildflowers and birds. Most important, there had been his private place, beneath a tangle of thorn and hazel. It could not be seen from the outside, but, once you had clambered down, it was a perfect "room", the brambles plaiting overhead to make a ceiling, the air full of a green twilight and smelling of leaves and earth. He had told only Alex about it, and they had brought stones in for chairs; it had been lovely when it was raining, so dry and secret, with the sound of water all around.

Later, Gabriel had developed a kind of theory about his relationship with the Irish countryside. Just as Vermeer's light-flooded interiors seemed really to be the interior of his mind, so were the West Cork fields an embodiment of some mystery, some inwardness, to which he could not give a name, but which he *felt*: in the light, in the glimpse of a stream flowing beneath ferns, in his secret "room", in the copse where that thorn had pierced his palm. He had never told anyone about his theory, how he felt that the fields, the slopes and woods, were a projection of his psyche into greenness. Nor could he tell the other truth, that nature had given him back some of what his parents had denied him: love of the outside world and of himself within it. He could not even put it into his paintings yet, this sweetness; it was too deep and private.

So Gabriel walked and dreamed. But finally, one Saturday morning, he looked into the mirror at his unshaven face and vague eyes and decided that he really had begun to look odd, like a real hermit. Enough was enough: he would clean himself up and walk into the village, that very evening.

Above the quiet fields the sky was lilac, with an opalescent lustre; a smoke of midges hovered about his head. "Hello, cows," he said to the mournful-looking cows, in order to practise being sociable. They gazed with their lugubrious eyes at him, before returning to their eternal dinner of grass.

In Ballycurry, music was spilling out of the pubs into the one curving road. Beyond the houses, the mountains had turned to mist in the radiant dusk, and in this uncertain light the whole village seemed to glow like an antique oil lamp.

Gabriel chose O'Driscoll's pub, because it was the quietest. It was an old-fashioned place, with a small shop offering sweets, Barry's tea, condensed milk and Batchelors peas, bags of Progress oatlets and boxes of pasta, all arrayed behind a plain wooden counter. The pub proper was at the back, an austere room presided over by the Misses O'Driscoll, Nora and Una. Although approaching eighty, both O'Driscoll sisters were astonishingly beautiful; Gabriel had wanted to paint them the moment he saw them, if only he were good at portraits.

Nora had immense eyes in a face moulded like a heart. She wore her russet-coloured hair, still abundant, gathered up with black combs. All in all, she resembled some vivid bird. Even her movements – quick and delicate – were birdlike.

Una's beauty was sterner. Her silver hair was cropped short, and she wore spectacles over her kindly eyes, which were an undimmed cornflower blue.

When Gabriel came into the pub this Saturday night, Una made a special effort to welcome him, extending her hand, and he realised that this was because the village had begun to accept him. When he'd first drunk at Nora and Una's, they had been courteous but distant. Now, he imagined, Mrs O'Carroll had told them how he was settling nicely into his grandfather's house, which had more or less lain idle since his great-uncle

died, except for an occasional tenant. She might even have
extolled his paintings to them. He'd let her see a couple of canvases, and she had clasped her hands to her breast in admira-
tion. Perhaps the O'Driscoll ladies were pleased that another
artist had settled in their midst. Anyway, Una was certainly
more friendly now than she'd been before.

"Good evening, boyeen," she said. "Fine weather we've been
having, thanks be to God."

"Yes, lovely. Though the midges are a bother."

"Indeed they are, and the flies as well, though I suppose we
shouldn't complain. Sure, when I was a small girl we had so
many rats it was a scandal." She gave a warm laugh. "I was a
fierce killer of rats, in my day!"

She excused herself to draw his pint of Murphy's, and while
she was gone he looked at his fellow drinkers: two burly farmers huddled at the bar, tweed coats buttoned up to the throat,
caps sloping over weather-beaten faces, despite the balmy
evening. One was smoking a pipe, the other talking in a soft,
urgent voice. Both were taking pints of stout with whiskey
chasers. A "crusty" couple occupied a bench in the corner,
smoking hand-rolled cigarettes and drinking half pints of cider.
At the table next to Gabriel's chair, two prosperous-looking,
middle-aged men, doubtless holidaymakers down from Cork,
were discussing Gaelic games and drinking red wine. Una
returned with Gabriel's pint, which looked delectable with its
ebony sheen beneath that circle of foam.

Settling on the chair next to him, she said, "I was talking this
morning with Kitty O'Carroll. She was going to ring you herself, but, sure, while you are here tonight I might as well tell

you. She said to me this morning that she will have to give up her job with yourself and with all the others she works for." Una tilted closer. "'Tis the heart. Doctor Henchy said she must rest, for she's had a heart problem since last Christmas, so he said, only she wasn't taking it seriously, and now it's coming against her."

"Oh, dear," Gabriel sighed. "What shall I do now?" Seeing Una's eyes narrow, he hastened, "How terrible for poor Mrs O'Carroll. I hope she improves." Then, after a tactful pause, he repeated, "What shall I do now, Una? Do you know anyone who might do a bit of housekeeping for me?"

She pursed her lips. "I wouldn't, boyeen, I wouldn't off-hand. But I will think about it and come up with someone."

She bustled away to attend to her other customers, leaving Gabriel to polish off his pint. He called for another, with a small whiskey beside it, like the two farmers.

He was idly listening to the Corkmen's conversation about hurling. They were probably barristers or doctors, with their contented smiles and ample stomachs. On the other hand, the one closer to Gabriel was wearing a blue blazer with brass buttons. Perhaps they were yachtsmen, moored at Ballybracken harbour. Anyway, whatever they were, Gabriel (by this time halfway down his third pint and second whiskey) had decided that they were bourgeois bores, typical enemies of the lonely artist – except if they were enlightened enough to buy his paintings.

"D'you mean that silly game they play with sticks here?" Gabriel addressed them, smiling. "That's not a real man's game. Nobody gets properly hurt, and they look as if they're playing with feather dusters!"

The two Corkmen looked up from their drinks, startled but still friendly. "And what in your estimation would be a real man's game, now?" asked one heartily. "Punching someone in the bread basket, like some of your big American boxers?"

Gabriel had never been one for sports, but he had glimpsed enough on television to talk with a pretence of authority. "Hurling is not in the same class as ice hockey," he declared. "You were talking about the speed of it, but in ice hockey the men crash into one another at one hundred miles an hour. Even with the helmets and leggings, they get badly hurt. Sometimes there's blood on the ice, if a puck goes wrong. Hurling is chicken feed, compared with that – a game for schoolgirls! Besides, the pair of you look too prosperous to play any sort of game yourselves."

He was dimly aware that a silence had fallen. Looking around, he noticed Nora at the counter, frozen in the process of clearing a spill, the white cloth clutched in her hand, her great blue eyes staring at him. Next he registered that the two farmers had swivelled their broad heads around to regard him. Like bulls, he thought, stupid bulls. The Corkmen, red-faced, had moved away and were gazing into their glasses while they continued to talk in low voices. Full of resentment and a sluggish misery, Gabriel acknowledged to himself that he'd said the wrong thing, again.

He took a gulp of whiskey, scalding his throat. He supposed that those men had reminded him of his father, with their genial smiles that could not temper something brutal in their eyes. Possibly, on some unconscious level, he had meant to insult them, since he was still wounded by his banishment. He mustn't forget that while he no longer loved his so-called family, there was still a voice in his head which he could not quash, the voice of the hurt, secretive child he had been: *Father, father, why have you abandoned me?*

On the other hand, surely it wasn't his fault if a couple of middle-class buffoons couldn't take a joke? And as for the others, who had stared at him, they were provincials, after all. Why was he letting them fluster him?

He remained on his chair, brooding. Irish music floated in from the pub across the road, the skirling of a flute with a *bodhrán* beneath. More people came in, speaking in the lilting accents of County Cork. They seemed to him rosy with pleasure, expansive, while he must look a sullen lump, drinking too much, all on his own. He decided at that moment to clear his head by befriending people as soon as possible, calling on his neighbours tomorrow; there was someone along his road called Tony Something, also a painter, from America. He would call on this Tony, and on Fleur Penhalligan, and on Farmer Coughlan and Farmer Coughlan's sister. If he had made a gaffe tonight it was doubtless because he had been too long immured in the empty farmhouse, and therefore this sudden swoop into village life had disconcerted him.

The pub was growing more and more crowded, as locals, tourists and well-dressed ex-pats poured in for an aperitif before going to dine at Fiona's Restaurant next door. Gabriel made to leave, but Una waylaid him, placing a hand on his arm.

"I won't forget," she said, "I will try to find someone to take Kitty O'Carroll's place for you."

He decided that he had been given a special dispensation

because he was a newcomer. The O'Driscoll sisters would not condemn him for his social awkwardness, at least not yet. He smiled his gratitude and strode out into the night.

•••

She had long dark hair, buoyantly curly, and fine eyebrows which were vividly black against the white skin of her forehead. Her eyes were light blue, wide and candid-looking, with long lashes. She had the round, rosy cheeks of an Edwardian poster girl: one could imagine her sporting a sailor's blouse and displaying a bottle of Coca-Cola.

While she walked through the house, he studied her. Her body in its lumpy jersey and jeans looked clumsy, too plump, but his instinct told him that hers was the kind of figure which was beautiful naked; that clothes – or at least modern clothes – could not flatter such old-fashioned curves and softnesses.

Her name was Charlotte, but he was to call her Lottie. This she announced on his threshold, at ten in the morning, extending an ink-spattered hand. Her accent was faintly American, though mostly Irish, with those melodious quaverings peculiar to Cork.

"Una O'Driscoll said you'd like some help about the house," she explained tersely, "so here I am." Then, defensively, "I'm *really* a writer, not a professional *housekeeper* or anything, but I need the money. I charge six quid an hour."

Mrs O'Carroll had charged only five. He hesitated, regarding her, that Gibson Girl face, those clear eyes, the full breasts beneath that appalling jersey. She was about twenty-three, he thought, and ripe as a plum.

"When can you begin?" he asked, putting on the kettle.

She settled at the kitchen table, looking blandly at him. "Any time. Right now, if you'd like, though I prefer to keep my mornings free, for my own work." She said this loftily, reminding Gabriel that she was very young and probably quite jejune. A writer, indeed! He decided that she was certainly too unseasoned by love or sorrow to write anything of merit: all she had were vigour and self-regard.

"What kind of writing do you do?" he asked indulgently, placing two cups of tea on the table.

"I'm a playwright, mainly, although at the moment I'm working on a book of poems." She curved her rather podgy and none-too-clean hands around one of the cups and slurped at the tea.

"Ah," replied Gabriel, still feeling indulgent. "And which playwrights do you admire? I mean, who would you say are your major influences?"

"Shakespeare, mainly."

He thought she couldn't be serious, but those large eyes were gazing levelly at him, without even a glint of irony. He said, "I see. And what do you like about Shakespeare, particularly?"

"Do you have any biscuits?"

He got up, put some shortbread on a plate and returned to the table. She extended her grubby little hand, seized two of the biscuits and proceeded to munch away at them, dropping crumbs all over her jumper.

"I like his sense of drama," she explained through a mouthful of shortbread. "And his characters are really interesting, although Cordelia is a bit of a wimp, and old Lady MacDeath is pretty exaggerated."

"Surely you mean Macbeth, Lottie?"

"I was *joking*." She gave him her flat blue stare. "Anyway, I haven't had anything produced yet, but there's plenty of time, and a lot of people have told me how talented I am. They say you're a painter."

He resisted an impulse to counter her naive self-praise with a description of his more serious accomplishments. He could tell her about his SoHo studio and the notices he had received in some of the local New York arts papers, but she might conclude that he was merely boasting. Better to respond to her callow swaggering with modesty and dignity. "Yes," he said simply, "along with others along this road, like Fleur Penhalligan."

She smiled in a slightly insolent way which reminded him, uncomfortably, of Ardyth. "Yeah, there are quite a few visuals living in West Cork. Some are better than others."

Choosing to ignore this, he asked about her background, and she told him that her parents, originally from Ballybracken, had tried to make a go of it in America, but it hadn't worked out. They had returned when she was ten, which explained her curious accent, West Cork with a vaguely American undercurrent. Even some of her diction was American.

Because he knew that his own accent was alloyed with Irish cadences and because of his own transatlantic past, he felt compelled to say, "I was also an international kid, living both in the States and here."

"Maybe," she said with that same insolent smile, "but you weren't like me. Your family were *rich*. Being poor is different. Anyway, I'd like to work for you, if you don't mind me coming in the afternoon. I could begin tomorrow?"

Again he regarded her, saying to himself that those guileless blue eyes and crimson cheeks were perhaps just an accident of physiognomy. They made her look innocent, but it had become clear in the course of this interview that she was actually quite sly and full of an undirected sensuality which both troubled and intrigued him.

"All right, Lottie," he agreed, grasping her plump hand. "It's a deal."

Chapter 5

BALLYCURRY LAY IN a pleat between low mountains, its single road unfurling upwards, house after gaily painted house. A mere fifteen hundred people lived there, swollen to two thousand each summer, and there were only a few hundred houses – yet the village supported twelve pubs. There was no chemist's shop or bank, as though such needs were irrelevant.

Tony liked to walk from the bird-thronged estuary at the bottom of the town, past the pubs, shops and houses, to the Catholic church which commanded the summit. From there, at dusk, he could gaze out at the mountains dissolving into a blue vapour or down at the village, that parade of houses painted yellow, green, lilac, red. He would marvel at the diversity of life in his adopted home: so many dreamers and vagabonds, rich and poor, had come to settle here. If he were to walk into O'Driscoll's pub, he might stumble into an English film director or a Swedish novelist, both of whom had bought houses near by. If, on the other hand, he chose MacCarthy's, he would meet up with a cluster of so-called crusties, relaxed and friendly, numerous children clutching at their legs. Keating's pub was favoured by the locals. (Tony never ceased to wonder that there *were* locals still living around Ballycurry.) Inside Keating's, in a kind of brownish gloom, farmers with wind-roughened faces, shopkeepers, builders – most wearing caps and wellingtons – would slouch at the bar, talking or dreaming into their pints; the air would smell of stout, damp wool and tobacco.

Neither a hippie nor a local, nor a wealthy ex-pat, and without any prejudices, Tony was welcome in all the pubs, and he liked them all. Yet, though highly emotional, he was not sentimental, so that a certain ruefulness tempered his love for Ballycurry. He was perceptive enough to recognise that Ireland's new prosperity was not entirely good for the village, that it was coarsening the attitudes of some Ballycurrians and endangering the beauty of the place. From the top of the town, he could see the new, American-style petrol station and some of the pallid bungalows which had begun to mushroom all along the way to Ballybracken.

Still, he did love it here. He loved the three-mile walk home from the village, past the Protestant church which seemed to drowse in a green smoke, its walls furred with moss and canopied with broad oaks. Hundreds of Huguenot settlers, Camiers, Merciers, Dukelows, were buried beneath its tombstones. Only a few houses stood beyond the church, all square nineteenth-century farmhouses, since his valley was isolated enough to have escaped, at least for the time being, the factory farms and the sprawl of holiday cottages so numerous elsewhere. He was happier here than he had ever been in any other place, perhaps because it was the region's custom to embrace people like himself, bohemian types, wanderers, artists and renegades, outsiders in general. And it was beautiful. Moved by these perspectives – so new to him – of rock, moor and ocean, he was beginning to paint in ways which sometimes delighted him, other times, as with the recent picture of the dawn and the cuckoo, unnerved him, somehow.

• • •

"Your stubborn hair, of which I am fond, has got impossibly shaggy," declared Fleur, brandishing a scissors. "Do bring me yesterday's *Irish Times* and a towel from the bathroom."

They spread the sheets of newspaper on the kitchen floor and put a chair on top of them. She draped the towel about his shoulders.

"Are you sure you're good at this?" he asked uneasily.

She gave him her wry look. "Tony, your hair is all unkempt anyway. I couldn't possibly make it worse. Just keep still."

She circled round him, scissoring away, her eyes narrowed in concentration. A gauze of hair tumbled over his face. Since she kept passing before him, he could not resist extending his hands to caress her hips and waist. "Stop, or I might slip and crop off your ear," she scolded.

"Then I could be a wounded genius, like Vincent."

Suddenly he was aware that they were not alone; someone had walked in through the open kitchen door. Fleur felt it, too; abruptly she froze, lowering the scissors, and turned round. Tony brushed the hair from his face.

A tall man was standing there, smiling. He was unusually handsome, with dark hair, startlingly pale almond eyes and broad shoulders. Tony felt a tremor of discomfort and wondered was it jealousy. He himself must look ridiculous, with his hair half-cut.

"I'm sorry if I'm intruding," said the man in a classy American accent, "but the door was open, and people around here are so friendly. . ." He made a helpless gesture. "So I thought I'd be bold and walk in. I only want to say hello, to introduce myself, since I'm your new neighbour."

He made this speech mostly to Fleur. Tony had seen the grey eyes take him in, then glide almost immediately to Fleur's puzzled face. *This guy's on the make*, he said to himself, in an American tough-guy argot he hadn't known he could muster. *This guy's an operator.*

Still looking puzzled, Fleur introduced herself, and the man answered in a rich, pleased voice, just as Tony guessed he would, "I *know* who you are, of course. It's lovely to meet you."

"And this poor shorn lamb is Tony," said Fleur, putting a hand – a rather too protective hand, Tony thought – on his shoulder.

"Ah, your son?" asked the stranger, with a probably unconscious impertinence. In fact, everything about him suggested impertinence: the cheeky way he had strolled in, obviously expecting to be welcomed, his insinuating smile. That he'd blundered into a private moment had not ruffled him in the least.

Fleur said equably, "No, Tony is my dear friend."

"Ah," repeated the man, giving Tony a brief smile. Then he told them his own name and where he was living. And then, in a solemn voice, he declared that he was an artist.

Does he want us to genuflect? thought Tony. He was praying that Fleur would not offer him a drink or a cup of tea.

But, "Thank you for dropping in," she said in her pleasant way. "We do hope you will enjoy living in Glenfern."

"I'm sure I will." The exotic eyes gleamed at her. *He thinks he's a real charmer*, Tony observed sullenly, *with those movie-star looks.*

After he had gone, Fleur resumed her work, circling round and round him, pruning intently; once more a silt of hair spilled over his face. For a while they were silent, then Tony ventured, "He was quite handsome, wasn't he?"

"Yes. Quite handsome."

"About thirty-five, I'd say."

"Mmm."

Another silence. Tony removed a piece of hair from his tongue. "He's probably very nice, wouldn't you think?"

"Possibly." He had closed his eyes against the shower of hair, but he sensed a quivering in her body, as though she were suppressing a sneeze or else laughing. He persisted, "Of course, you have to like those particular kind of looks, to consider him handsome."

"Oh? And what are his particular kind of looks?"

"The *vain* kind. The spoilt, presumptuous, *vain* kind."

"You may open your eyes."

Her fingers brushed the hair from his face. Then she brought him a hand mirror. They both regarded his reflection. He thought his hair looked the same, only tidier. He stared at himself, and himself stared glumly back. Presently Fleur said, "You look lovely, darling."

She settled on his knee, putting her arms around his shoulders. She was openly laughing now. "You needn't be concerned about that man," she said sternly. "I recognised what he was the moment I saw him. Don't you see? He can't help revealing precisely what he wants to conceal – his very effort exposes him."

Tony realised, sheepishly, that he had underestimated her. Of course she was not deceived by that visitor. She was used to petitioners, to aspirants of every hue. Hundreds of would-be artists, from the genuinely gifted to the self-deluding, must have come to her door throughout the years, appealing for a benediction from the famous Fleur Penhalligan.

"Feeling better?" she asked, still half-laughing.

"He was pushy and awful," Tony muttered, but he *was* feeling better.

She said in a thoughtful voice, "One mustn't be too hard on people like that, although we shouldn't let them get too close. After all, the real reason we dislike them is that they remind us of ourselves, those places in ourselves where we are insecure and clumsy. We don't like to be reminded of our own desperation."

He thought about how he had felt after his Dublin girlfriend rejected him. He had been doing a series of bird paintings, and during the period when he was at the very crux of his grief, writhing with misery on his solitary bed, he'd painted a bird who could not fly, who dragged its feathers in the dust, shorn of power, feeding on bits of refuse. "No," he said slowly, "no, we don't like to be reminded of our desperation."

Suddenly he was more aware than usual of the age difference between them. She was an accomplished artist and a mature

woman, while he was gauche and juvenile. As though to banish
these thoughts, he put his hand inside her blouse and touched
her breast. She wound her arms more tightly about him, and
they kissed.

For some reason which he could not fathom, he was her
elder here, in the realm of physical love. When they made love
it was he who was confident, while she opened to him shyly,
almost anxiously. And this tremulousness of hers never ceased
to inflame him – it made him want to crush and protect her at
the same time. Always, after he had touched and kissed her for
a while, she would finally abandon herself, and then he would
grow nearly crazy with passion. Now (after prudently closing
the door), he made love to her on the kitchen floor. They rolled
about, oiled with sweat, yesterday's *Irish Times* and bits of his
hair sticking to their skin; he half-consciously saw an ad for
Avonmore soups and an editorial about the ceasefire.

The balance of age and youth had been righted, he thought.

• • •

At dusk they walked out to her small greenhouse, to gather
tomatoes for a salad. Within the glass panels, the smell of soil
and spring tomatoes was heady.

He carried the full basket, and she walked lightly before him,
back towards the house. Bundles of lavender cloud were gliding across a mother-of-pearl sky, and the garden had grown
dark and quiet except for the flutterings, here and there, of a
thrush or swallow. They walked under the apple trees, which
were tarnished with lichen, their leaves a black filigree against
those lilac clouds. Suddenly she turned to him; he put the basket on the ground. Her face was in shadow. "Tony," she said

softly, "I didn't like that man intruding today. He frightened me, a bit."

"I know. It made me feel afraid to leave you on your own here. Meanwhile, we'll have to remember to close up all the doors and windows. Isn't that an awful thought, as though Glenfern were London or New York, or even Dublin!"

She touched his face with her cool fingers. He kissed her, then said impulsively, "I do so love making love to you, but sometimes I'm troubled by feelings. . ." He drew a breath. "Sometimes I'm troubled by my fantasies. You are so sweet, and so timid in bed–"

"Ought I to be more aggressive?"

It was too dark to read her expression. "No! I love how you are. It excites me how you are so . . . so at my mercy, if you know what I mean. Is that wrong to say?"

She was quiet a moment, then began to speak in a careful, storytelling voice. "My family were very strict, very low-church, not at all easy with sex, as you can imagine. My father was all right, really, just rather stern, but my mother was either terribly aloof or else she would punish us – my sister and me – quite harshly, often for trivial things, like spilling the milk at table, ordinary things."

She paused again, then resumed more softly, "Once, a few years ago, I was alone here, painting. It was evening and very quiet, and I was concentrating so hard, it was as though I'd been spirited to another world. Suddenly, there was a crash – a bottle or something had toppled down on the counter, and the sound was loud as a gunshot in the stillness – I nearly jumped in the air. . ." She gave a low laugh. "Of course I had been startled, but I realised at once that what I had also felt, when that crash shattered the quiet, was a *frisson*, a sexual *frisson*. It had been like that, you see, in my parents' house, when I or my sister displeased our mother. It had been the same thing, stillness, then a sudden cry – unexpected, extreme – and my sister and I would feel a tingling in our blood, a not unpleasant excitement, even when we were afraid. . ."

He said, "But is it wrong? Is it wrong to indulge these fantasies? I sometimes pretend that I'm forcing you, that I'm a rough farmer like old Coughlan and I've got you pressed up against the wall and you're resisting, but then you give in, and I call you all kinds of names."

"Does it excite you, that fantasy?" She was moving her fingers over his face, his brow and cheekbones, the curve of his jaw, as though she were trying to see him with her fingers.

"Yes! But I wonder–"

A young rabbit stared at them from the border of the orchard, its ears alert, before jumping silently back into the growing darkness. "In love," she murmured, "all is permitted. These fantasies are so deep in us, so primordial. Why shouldn't we journey into them, with our beloved?"

"It isn't playing with fire?"

"I don't know." She pressed herself against him, and he buried his face in her hair. Her head on his shoulder, she went on, "But if we are travelling into the heart of ourselves, into our own mystery, with someone who allows us to explore *everything*, even the things we are ashamed of, and who also reveals those same places in himself. . . Then it is a voyage towards consciousness, isn't it?"

He did not answer. The garden was cool now, and it was too dark to see her face. Suddenly, he pushed her down on to the orchard floor and kissed her roughly. "Don't move," he ordered.

She lay still; he could just make out her hair, a pale flurry against the grass, and a gleam of teeth from her half-open mouth. He slid off her knickers and began to touch her in the ways he knew would drive her mad. "Don't move," he repeated sternly.

"But I–"

"I know you want to, but if you don't lie perfectly still, I'll stop."

"Don't stop." A whisper.

"Then don't move."

She was rigid, breathing heavily; he knew that this was torture for her but also bliss. He could feel, under his fingers, her body's tension, its *need* to move in concert with his hand; she was thrumming beneath the skin. But, "Don't move," he commanded again, and she obeyed.

There was a smell of bruised grass, of last year's mouldering apples, of tomatoes, of resin. Suddenly she cried, "I can't, oh, I can't," and then she came with a cry and a long, shuddering paroxysm.

• • •

A few evenings later, Tony and Fleur decided to walk into town, for a drink at O'Driscoll's pub. It had been a dullish day, but towards seven o'clock the sky quickened with sunlight, while cloud-shadows glided like giant birds over the flanks of the mountains. It was just too lovely to stay at home.

As usual, the pub was full, mostly of people like themselves, artists of the ex-pat variety, as well as a few tourists. Three small children were chattering to Una and Nora, who tilted down to caress their heads and press sweets on them.

Someone walked over to speak to Fleur and Tony, a man whom they knew and liked. He was a distinguished, elderly Englishman, a translator of classical Greek plays, called Aubrey Bellowes. He had the attenuated face of a tomb effigy; one could nearly picture him moulded in stone with a dog at his feet, beneath an ancient banner decaying to a cobweb. He had long silver hair and smoked a pipe. Rumour had it that he had been a "rogue" in his youth, before marrying happily, rather late in life. He had settled in Ballycurry about a decade ago, after his wife's death. In the town he was known to follow a civilised if unexacting ritual: lunch in the bookshop-café, supper at home, then two or three cognacs at O'Driscoll's before bed.

"Good evening, my dear," he said to Fleur, "and to you, young friend." He settled beside them with his glass of brandy and announced that he was rereading the *Odyssey*, and that it never ceased to move him, even though he knew it so well.

"I am at the sirens bit," he told them, "where Odysseus, fearing the fatal cries of the sirens, orders his men to stop up their ears." He made a flourishing motion with his pipe in the air. "But, as you know, Odysseus keeps his own ears open."

"Doesn't he order his men to bind him up with ropes?" asked Fleur.

"Indeed. Yet he *listens*. He might restrain himself, but he chooses experience, to hear and to understand, even though he knows that those voices will torment him to near madness.

Marvellous story, isn't it? I believe it is a wonderful metaphor for the journey into consciousness, which, as we know, all responsible people should try to undertake."

Tony was astonished by this last phrase, so uncannily like Fleur's, only a few days ago. Aubrey continued, "We all have our sirens, or as Jung put it, our "shadow" side. Many people either flee from their own shadow, or else they are seduced by it. Either way, they live at its mercy. It seems to me that Odysseus had the right idea. One should try to understand it, without succumbing to its dark attractions. After all, one cannot recognise angels if one refuses to see devils." He asserted this last point in his pedantic yet endearing way, with another flourish of his pipe.

He took his leave of them then, and Tony and Fleur talked on for a while, their fingers interlaced beneath the table. Tony was thinking about his own sirens, his dreams of a chaste Fleur made wanton with lust, a haughty Fleur degraded, sultans and harems, ravishment, perversions: all the comic opera of desire. He looked at her – those thoughtful fawn eyes – and remembered how melancholy, almost haggard, she had looked when he first saw her. That tired expression was entirely gone now. As for himself, he no longer felt so gawky: he was growing easy in his own skin.

A painting began to take shape in his imagination, an image of the bound Odysseus, only his own Odysseus would not be restrained with ropes. Tony pictured a strong body aching with some monumental effort, the cables of its throat and arms like internal restraints, and, overlaying this figure, other, less distinct figures, almost ghostly. Excited by this image, he squeezed

Fleur's hand, thinking that she had brought him the possibility of better work than he had yet done.

Chapter 6

SURPRISINGLY, LOTTIE WAS a good cook. Every evening, before cycling home, she left a meal for him, as Mrs O'Carroll had done, only Lottie's dishes were more inventive: an aromatic curry, a *pot-au-feu*, a sauté of prawns and vegetables. On the fourth day, he suggested that she remain late and eat with him.

He wasn't sure why he proposed this; in fact he wasn't sure how he felt about her in general. For three days she had bustled almost silently about his house, cleaning up efficiently, but always with a sullen expression. He gathered that she resented the menial nature of her job and therefore resented him. In her adolescent way, she had decided she was a writer; why should she be scrubbing the toilet of some rich Yank? So she worked well, but in a miasma of surly gloom which was oppressive to him. And he was further oppressed by her unfocused sensuality, by the way her grubby clothes contrasted with her beautiful, blooming face, by the way those same clothes – unravelling

jumpers, drooping jeans – failed to do justice to her opulent
figure. It was as though she wore such unfortunate get-ups
expressly to camouflage her voluptuousness, but, on the other
hand, there was always something slyly sexual in her manner.
Even her moroseness was somehow charged in this way, as
though she were for ever giving him a sidelong look, challeng-
ing him.

When he asked her to dine with him, she muttered, "I left
you a small roast beef. It isn't large enough for two. Besides, I'm
not hungry."

"I see. Perhaps tomorrow, then?"

She was staring down at her feet. "Maybe." Suddenly she
looked at him. "Listen, could I have a bath, before I go? My
immersion heater broke this week, and there's no hot water."

He regarded her dishevelled hair and smudged hands. The
prospect of a cleaned-up Lottie was not unappealing.

"Of course. I always have hot water."

She grunted a barely audible "thanks". He made to get her a
towel from the hot press, but she said brusquely, "Don't bother. I know where they are. I work here, remember?" Really, he
thought, the girl was appallingly rude. Before disappearing into
the bathroom, she gave him a cool look from those round blue
eyes, along with a small smile which he could not read.

Listening to the muffled cascade of water into the bath, he felt
vaguely irritated, as though he had been rebuked somehow, put
in his place. But what he done except generous things, asking her
to eat with him – he would have opened a bottle of good wine –
and allowing her to have a bath? She was just a sulky little bitch;
he shouldn't let her discomfit him. Nevertheless he was at a loss

now, unable to concentrate. The deep evening light was lovely; he should be working in his studio, or reading, but an invisible magnet seemed to keep him captive in the kitchen, where, restive, annoyed, he walked fruitlessly about, listening to the splashing sounds from the bathroom. Presently he poured himself a whiskey.

After about thirty minutes she emerged, wearing nothing but the towel. Her shoulders, pearled with water, looked nearly iridescent, and her wet hair clung in blue-black scrolls to them; a tendril was caught in the velvet space between her breasts, only half-covered by his towel. She gazed at him with her customary wide-eyed stare, half-bland, half-brazen.

His mouth felt suddenly parched. Trying to speak casually, he said, "You haven't dried yourself properly."

"Maybe you could do a better job."

Again, he was eerily reminded of Ardyth, of her probably conscious *film noir* witticisms, when she had stood half-naked in his loft, in a previous existence. Was he destined to tangle himself up with such women for ever, to be enticed over and over into the webs of arch sirens who confused their hardheartedness with sophistication, smiling their snide smiles at him? Despite his desire, he was almost weary as he took the towel from her and languorously passed it over the lush breasts, their nipples hard and red as haws, the supple arms, the full hips, the glossy black curls between her thighs, weary, as though he had followed this script too many times and knew the story's outcome all too well.

She kissed him, and he was glad she'd had the bath; she smelled so clean and young. They made love on the sofa; or perhaps making love was too gentle a term for it. Her body was as lovely and luscious as he'd suspected, but even while he moved his hands and lips over her white flesh, it occurred to him that this intimacy between them was dangerous, because essentially they did not like each other. Their physical closeness would not be sweetened by tenderness; when he was spent inside her he would not love her, nor would she love him. What they *were* feeling was lust, coarsened with contempt, and he'd have felt soiled if she weren't so good at sex, so bold and hungry.

About two hours later, while she was putting on her ragged clothes – the butterfly transformed back into a caterpillar – he drowsily asked her, from his supine position on the sofa, would she like a drink before leaving?

"No. I want to get home." So she was just Lottie again, discourteous, mulish, as though nothing had happened between them. He wondered if she expected him to offer her more money, for her extra services.

But she merely mumbled a goodbye and went wheeling off home on her blue bicycle. She had told him that she lived in the middle of Ballycurry, in a flat above Mrs Hackett's food shop, where, he presumed, she laboured at her Shakespeare-inspired masterpieces when she wasn't working for him or drinking with her pals at O'Driscoll's pub.

After she'd gone, he felt melancholy and was annoyed with himself for feeling melancholy; it was such a cliché, those famous glooms which are supposed to descend on one after love. But, of course, it was not love; whatever he and that surly urchin had engaged in, it was not love. And yet it had resembled love, the ghost of love had been couched in it. It had been like living in a barren place and hearing distant echoes from a happier country. He had never known that country, could barely conceive of it. But he and Lottie had behaved as though they'd arrived there, had kissed and explored each other like genuine lovers.

He walked to the window and stared out at the night. The fields were flooded with a bloodless glow of moonlight, and the sky was an inverted chalice of light: that nearly full moon, bright as a lamp, with scarves of cloud floating across it, and manifold stars. Yes, they'd gone through the motions, but it had been a pantomime, and therefore it had only deepened his loneliness. Yet he knew he would do it again. He wouldn't be able to resist her succulent body and feral appetite. What a cynic he was!

He was remembering a passage about Botticelli from Vasari's *Lives of the Artists*, that book which had been his solace as a child. Always exuberantly anecdotal, Vasari had written that Botticelli's father, impressed by the boy's determination, apprenticed him to Fra Filippo Lippi, in whose studio he flourished. Such love, thought Gabriel now, such belief in a son, so remarkable that a stern Italian father from a sterner, more formal period in history should alter his expectations, swallow his misgivings about the impractical nature of such a life and allow his son to become an artist. Against the night sky, Gabriel conjured up Botticelli's women, the serene ovals of their faces emerging from plumes and swirls of hair, their surprisingly lavish bodies, naked or clothed in clinging robes, breasts and haunches as ample as Lottie's.

Suddenly he began to weep dryly – harsh sobs without tears. He was gifted, he knew it, but the thought had come to him that his gift might not flower. Maybe they had blighted him for ever. He closed his eyes; he was coming close to the heart of his pain, that lonely source, a little boy standing in a copse while birds clatter overhead. . . If the inner life were indeed a secret wood, then his parents lived in its shallowest corners. He longed to explore its depths, but they had taught him "good" manners without giving him anything, any beauty or mystery, with which to replace his impulses. Yet he knew that a kind of beauty must exist inside himself; it had become his sustaining dream. Why shouldn't he become a great artist? Why not? Why not? He felt genuinely baffled, was intelligent enough to realise that he was missing something, but could not, for the life of him, figure out what the secret might be. He thought mainly in terms of manipulating or charming those with power. He did not think often about the problem of painting his nature vision, believing remotely that such paintings would "come" to him, somehow, after he had achieved success and was less vulnerable to criticism.

In the meantime, he would return to the kitchen and polish off that bottle of whiskey.

• • •

Next day, Lottie arrived promptly and worked with her usual efficiency. And, also as usual, she was gruff when he spoke to her, averting her head, answering with nothing more than grunts or mutters. He was somewhat relieved; of course, their relationship was different now: he knew he could expect her to come into his arms again that evening. But the fact that she was her old self at all other times meant that on a practical level they could go on as before, which certainly suited him. She did not allude even by look or gesture to their lovemaking, and he guessed that this was a matter of pride to her. Pride for her and convenience for him. Everything was working out nicely, as it should.

But he was conscious, more than ever, of her presence, and when she came into the studio with his afternoon coffee and he registered yet again those long-lashed eyes and that lush figure, he could not concentrate. So he decided to go out for a walk instead.

Mr Coughlan was pruning the fuchsia at the entrance to his farm. On previous walks, Gabriel had noticed how industrious he was, in an old-fashioned way: whitewashing his byre, driving in the cows with a dog and a long stick, watering his small flower garden, even though he was quite ancient. His spinster sister was also elderly, eighty at least, Gabriel surmised, but he presumed that she worked just as hard in her own domain; it was she who would bake the brown soda bread every day and clean the house and wash their clothes.

He paused to say hello to Mr Coughlan, whose ruddy face made him think of apples, and to engage in the ritual Irish exchange about the weather: "Grand day, thanks be to God." Then Coughlan invited him into the house to greet his sister; the old man seemed glad of company.

Walking up to their door, Gabriel was struck by how simple and tidy everything looked. The chalk-white byre, the vivid flowers, the peach-coloured house with its curtained windows seemed more like a farm in Greece or Italy than here in modern

Ireland. He could imagine a woman swathed in black from head to foot, crow-like against that white byre, on a chair with her spindle, as one might see in Naples or Crete. Instead, he was welcomed at the scullery door by thin Miss Coughlan, with her pleasant blue eyes and blue apron.

"You'll have a whiskey," Farmer Coughlan declared as they entered the kitchen. It was a large plain room, with a lino floor, an oilcloth-covered table and a stout Stanley range. Blue delph glinted inside the china cabinet, and the walls were adorned with a Sacred Heart of Jesus above a votive lamp and an endearingly young-looking Blessed Virgin. Gabriel received a general impression of cleanliness and frugality; it was as though he had been spirited back in time, except for the television in the corner. Once, his own kitchen, and Fleur Penhalligan's, had looked like this.

As if reading his mind, Farmer Coughlan said, "Did you know, we are the only remaining people of our name in this valley? Our cousin Brighid was the last to pass away, four years ago. That young dark man, that painter from America, is living in Brighid's house now."

Gabriel felt unreasonably nettled to hear Tony Daly described as "that painter from America", but he was distracted by Miss Coughlan, who had come back from the pantry with two slender glasses so full of whiskey there was no room for water.

Handing one each to Gabriel and her brother, she said, "The day after Brighid's funeral, I was walking along Glenfern road. It was a summer afternoon like today, mild and bright. And then the strangest thing happened." She settled into a rocking chair, folding her hands composedly over the blue apron. "As I was walking, I heard voices, loud echoing voices. They seemed to be coming from the mountains. I stopped dead in the road, and even the cows and sheep stood still and lifted their heads. I heard a woman's voice – sobbing, so it was – and a number of men's voices that I thought were praying. Sure, I hurried home then."

Farmer Coughlan said, "She was white as milk coming in through that door. We rang our cousin in Ballybracken, to ask was there a regatta or something on, with loudspeakers that might echo over the mountains. But there was nothing. Then we knew that those voices were the valley itself, mourning. You see, our people had lived here for hundreds of years." He took a gulp of whiskey and laughed. "I suppose you wouldn't hear this class of thing in America. Sure, maybe you think we are just old and beginning to dote, with our *pisogues* and fairy talk, what you people would call baloney."

"No. I am awed," answered Gabriel, with an uncharacteristic simplicity. He was indeed awed: although it was hard for him to enter imaginatively into other people's stories, he was able to feel moved if their experience bore out his own. And the Coughlans' account confirmed his belief that the Irish earth harboured mysteries. Yet he was faintly embarrassed as well, because close exchanges were more or less foreign to him. Ever since his early life he had been wary of deep friendships; even he and Ardyth had seldom discussed their pasts, never their secrets. So while realising that he had been honoured by this confidence, he was not sure how to react. Anyway, as evening approached, it was hard for him to think about anything but Lottie.

He polished off his whiskey, which was giving him a nice glow. "Do you know a girl called Lottie Curran?" he asked bluntly. "She works for me, as my housekeeper."

"I would know her," replied Farmer Coughlan, tilting back in his chair. "She would be the daughter of Joseph Curran who is now dead. He was a hard-drinking man but hard-working as well. A decent enough man, though a biteen rough in his manners."

"Just like his daughter," said Gabriel wryly.

• • •

Tony Daly was exhibiting at the gallery in Ballybracken, Lottie announced. Would Gabriel like to take her to the opening?

At first he thought this might be a gesture of affection, until, with one of her sour looks, she explained, "I haven't a car, and Ballybracken is too far to cycle."

He consented, not from an impulse of chivalry towards Lottie, but because he was curious about this Tony Daly, curious and slightly vexed. Surely he was too young to be given a show at the Ballybracken, a prestigious gallery despite its remote location, or perhaps because of it, since West Cork had become so *chic* recently. Also, how had such a gangly, raw-boned creature managed to install himself in the bed of Fleur Penhalligan? The first and only time Gabriel had seen Tony, he had looked ridiculous with his bedraggled hair and that towel around his shoulders, but a few enquiries had established that he and Fleur were indeed lovers. Everyone in Ballycurry knew everything about one another; surely they knew that Lottie was doing more for him than his laundry, these days. Yet no one was shocked. The locals were so used to outsiders, to mavericks, to impoverished artists and merchant princes, to Continental tourists and crusty encampments, that they had grown tolerant as Parisians when it came to eccentric erotic behaviour.

As for Gabriel, he, too, was not shocked by the union between Fleur and Tony, merely piqued that he hadn't got there first. Certainly his personal charms were greater, although that boy's large brown eyes might appeal to a certain kind of sentimental woman. Anyway, it struck him as unfair that this unprepossessing twenty-five-year-old nobody should have an artist like Fleur Penhalligan as his lover *and* an exhibition in the hot new Ballybracken Gallery. Perhaps he was talentless, and Fleur had used her influence to arrange his show? Gabriel would like to see for himself.

• • •

There was quite a crowd at the gallery, and the abundance of free wine was making everyone flushed and vivacious. As soon as they arrived, Lottie stalked off on her own, as though to establish that they were not a couple. His eye followed her as she moved heavily about the room; he'd never seen her in public before. What a forlorn little guttersnipe she was, with that awful jumper.

Perhaps it was seeing her among people for the first time, but suddenly he understood what he should have realised long before: Lottie's moroseness was a defense against disappointment. She'd had to surrender her innocence too early. Something or someone must have wounded her when she was still very young, so that now she felt compelled to armour herself with that sullen air, with arrogance and those slovenly clothes. Perhaps, underneath, she was merely shy or melancholy. She

certainly looked lonely now, walking doggedly from painting
to painting, speaking to no one.

He supposed that he and she were alike in some ways, which
was why they were also a bit hostile to each other. This hostil-
ity spiced up their sex life; they liked to play rough, which was
thrilling, but it made him uneasy as well. Lust combined with
dislike was precisely the incendiary and poisonous brew he'd
known it would be, but he couldn't help disliking her. She was
humourless and boring, and her manners were disgusting. Yet,
also as he'd predicted, he couldn't resist her in bed. She was daring and wicked, would let him have her any way he pleased,
and she would do the same, would take command, straddle
him, use him for her own pleasure. It was all very exciting, but
it was perilously close to the precipice he had fallen over with
Ardyth, and he was apprehensive.

Gabriel averted his eyes from the paintings; he wanted to
sound the room first, register who was here and who absent and
how they were responding to both the pictures and each other.
There was Fleur, looking quite comely in a white dress, her hair
rippling about her shoulders. He noticed that her eyes were an
unusual fawn colour, like amber or butterscotch. She was certainly far more elegant than anyone else present, in a rather old-
fashioned way, evoking Pre-Raphaelite heroines. He felt
irrationally annoyed that he did not know her, since he and she
were surely kindred spirits, the two of them urbane and talented, as opposed to the local bumpkins, the bourgeois "blow-ins",
the unwashed crusties and that clumsy Tony Daly.

He observed that the airy room was thronged with ex-pats,
mostly of the prosperous variety; the only locals he recognised

were an elderly couple who kept a bakery in Schull, Seamus O'Sullivan of O'Sullivan's food shop and, surprisingly, the Ballycurry policeman, Garda Caffrey, in mufti. How strange, Gabriel thought, that a rural Irish garda should be interested in art, but, on the other hand, Ireland was a surprising country. Caffrey was tall, fair, with level features and vigilant eyes. He seemed kindly enough, but Gabriel felt uncomfortable in the presence of any policeman. After he had injured Ardyth, the New York cops had been brutish, handling him roughly, threatening him, asking oafish questions about his "history of violence". And then, a few evenings ago, he had been standing in his own garden, marvelling at how the twilight was *silver* – a lucent smoke above the mountains – when Garda Caffrey drove by, on patrol. He had said hello in an affable way, but Gabriel was made uneasy by those calm eyes, which had seemed to be measuring him.

Now, ignoring Garda Caffrey and everyone else and seizing a glass of wine, he finally noticed Tony, surrounded by admirers and looking insufferably pleased with himself. Gabriel debated whether he should speak to him or not, then decided to look at the pictures first.

There is a time of evening when the fields are darker than the sky, when a pale light blanches the clouds, and against this light the trees are black, the mountains smoke. *What is it called?* Gabriel asked himself. *What is the word for that milky evening light?* Then it came to him: *nacreous.* The canvas he was regarding was full of a nacreous glow, which seemed to encompass all the elements. At first he thought he was looking at a seascape, then clouds, then a field. There were vague figures in the background, green and scarlet, done with a paint-heavy brush, and perhaps a cottage, its windows gold with lamplight. Gabriel's throat contracted; suddenly he was smelling verdure, that smell of hawthorn and fern which the fields breathe after rain. He turned away.

He gulped down his wine and took another glass from the table. Moving aside, he nearly stumbled into Fleur.

"Sorry," he said, righting himself immediately and giving her his very best smile. "Didn't mean to jostle you, but it's crowded in here, isn't it?"

"Yes. Quite a successful opening," she declared, and he saw that she was feeling happy – and proud. Proud of that pipsqueak Daly! Unable to banish a dryness from his voice, he observed, "His work is rather *misty*, wouldn't you say? A bit romantic?"

Her eyes, gazing at him, seemed to darken to a chestnut colour. "Yes, some of Tony's paintings are misty. His technique makes them glow with a misty light. They are very good indeed."

"Oh, he's promising, no doubt. And he's right to use oils. I do, myself. They are so luminous, far more interesting than acrylics, for example. I think I've used every kind of medium possible, in my own career, even tempera. My own work–"

Seamus O'Sullivan, his face shining with wine and excitement, descended on Fleur. He was a large, blunt-spoken man whose eyes managed to look at once sincere and shrewd – like Lottie's, Gabriel thought resentfully: perhaps that look was a Ballycurry characteristic, a kind of peasant cunning? "Grand pictures, Mrs York," Seamus cried, "though, sure, I know nothing about art. Would you ever explain–"

She smiled at Gabriel. "Won't you excuse me?"

He mustered an "of course", and drank down his wine. It was only plonk, but at least it was free. Anyway, he would rather drink than look at Tony's mawkish paintings, over which Fleur Penhalligan was making such an unnecessary fuss. Reaching for another glass, he noticed Tony himself, standing on his own for once.

Gabriel gestured to the wine table, and Tony smiled yes, he would like some of the red.

"Congratulations," Gabriel cried, brandishing his glass in a toast.

"Thanks," replied Tony absentmindedly, surveying the room. "You know, I was just wondering why so many of us – so many painters, I mean – have settled here. Fleur and myself, and you, among lots of others. Why is it that Ballycurry has become such a visual arts colony, almost exclusively, as opposed to an enclave for writers, say, or composers? Why aren't there more novelists and poets down here?"

Gabriel indicated Lottie in a corner of the room, slurping at a glass of wine and talking to a bearded man.

"That girl over there is a writer. She's my housekeeper. Among other things." He gave Tony a significant smile, but the man merely said, "I see. What does she write?"

"Plays, she says, and poetry. But it seems to me that her real talents lie elsewhere." Once more he smiled conspiratorially, but again Tony seemed not to comprehend, or else his politely blank look was a deliberate rebuff. At that moment, as though she had divined that they were talking about her, Lottie walked over, extending a podgy hand.

"Hi, I'm Lottie. I just wanted to say that your stuff is really great."

With some displeasure, Gabriel observed that her sullenness had been supplanted by a vivacity which he'd never seen in her before. She was fluttering her lashes and dimpling like a coy maiden.

Tony said courteously, "I hear you are a writer, Lottie."

Her eyes had fastened on him like headlamps; she didn't even glance over at Gabriel. "Yeah. I'm doing poems right now. Are you interested in poetry? Maybe you'd like to come over one day, to look at my work?"

Gabriel was pleased to see Tony blush. *The pair of them!* he thought bitterly. *She's a star-fucker, and he gets crimson as an adolescent.*

Tony said, "Thanks, but I'm very busy these days. If you posted them to me, I would be glad to read them, but I don't really know enough about poetry to be able to help you. Perhaps you should consult another poet, who could encourage you the way painters do for each other." He made a sheepish gesture in Gabriel's direction. "We were just saying that so few writers have come to live in these parts, as opposed to visual artists. I suppose we painters are lucky, having one another to talk to. Please excuse me. I must speak to that guy in the corner; I think he might want to buy a picture!"

They gazed at his retreating back; then Gabriel clutched her arm, hard. "Come on, Lottie, I'm taking you home."

She narrowed her eyes at him, like an angry cat, but did not protest.

They drove through the moonless night in an acrid silence.

When he stopped the car at her door, she muttered, "You don't *own* me."

"I have no desire to own you. But when you behave like a trollop and make a fool of yourself in public, it embarrasses me. I ferried you there and brought you home, and you weren't even courteous enough to—"

"I didn't do anything. I was just curious. I mean, I don't know why he likes her. She's so old."

She was staring out the window, so that all he could see of her was the curve of her cheek and her tumble of curls, lustrous in the glow of a street lamp.

"I see," he said coldly. "You were intending to tutor him in young love? For your information, Fleur is not old. She looks about thirty-five, or perhaps forty, around my own age, anyway, and she is quite gifted. To tell you the truth, I don't know what *she* sees in *him.*"

Out in the road, the last of the drunks were shuffling home from the pubs, which had closed themselves up firmly, like sealed boxes. As the men passed his car, lurching along in their wellingtons, Gabriel smelled whiskey, sweat, pipe-smoke and buttermilk. He stared at Lottie, whose all-too-knowing baby-doll eyes stared back. There was something in the car with them, crackling between them, but whether it was lust or anger he did not know.

She said, "Want to come up to my place?"

She had only a lumpy single bed, but they made good use of it. At one point he did something ruthless to her, without preparing her, so that she screamed in pain.

But afterwards she said she had liked it.

Chapter 7

TONY HAD LOVED spring in Glenfern, the slopes burnished with gorse, a lace of bluebells along the hedges, newborn lambs burrowing under their mothers for milk. But now it was high summer and beautiful in a different way, all colour and scent, the air lazy with flies. Ballybracken harbour was warm enough to bathe in.

The ceasefire remained unbroken. On the evening news there were always interviews: a haggard man from the Shankill, wearing a rumpled raincoat, kneading a black hat in his hands, saying, "We never wanted any trouble, we were only trying to protect our communities. Hereabouts, we were all brought up with violence, but now we're right sick of it."

The interviewer asked, "Do you think there will be a lasting peace?"

The man's eyes widened. He seemed earnest. "Only if the Nationalists respect DEMOCRACY. The majority of the people of Northern Ireland want the Union to SURVIVE."

Tony and Fleur, two outsiders, were fascinated by these

glimpses. They ate dinner on her sofa, gazing at the television, and then, before bed, he would lie on the same sofa with his head in her lap, her hand rhythmically caressing his hair, while they absorbed the late-night discussion programmes.

One evening, RTÉ trundled their cameras into a pub on Sandy Row. Tony was struck by its name, the Orange Lily, and the decor – bowlers, sashes and photographs of the Royal Family – a display of Protestant kitsch eerily like the burly popes, Sacred Hearts and Blessed Virgins he was used to seeing in local farmhouses. And he was moved by the grizzled face of a man at the bar who was being asked his opinion of the cease-fire. It seemed a fatuous question. The man answered in staccato sentences. His daughter aged five, killed by the IRA, caught in crossfire, his marriage broken up. With an unexpected dignity, in a voice empty of self-pity, he concluded, "I have had a sad life."

"What age would you say he is?" asked Tony.

"Old before his time," Fleur answered wryly.

And now the man, face furrowed, was talking about Christ, forgiveness.

But the camera cut abruptly to the head and shoulders of another man, sombre-looking, above the legend, "Former IRA Activist". "In the North we are all victims."

The interviewer seized on the word "victim", contested it, then asked coldly, "Do you regret having killed people?"

"In war there are casualties. But enough is enough."

Tony watched intently as the scene moved to the grounds of the Maze prison where the wife of a Loyalist prisoner was being interviewed.

She looked suspiciously at the camera, a stout woman with small, watery eyes. "I'm sure Ireland is a very nice place, but I've no desire to go there."

• • •

In the hot afternoons they lay without clothes on a blanket in a concealed part of her garden. She reclined on her back, a hand under her head, gazing up at the sky, while he painted her in watercolours.

He liked how they complemented each other as painters. Fleur was renowned for her cool abstracts, but, even when venturing into abstraction, Tony never utterly abandoned the representational; there was always the suggestion of a house, a road, a field in his work. And, regularly, he returned to the figure, as now, balancing the heavy paper on his knees, looking and looking at her. She was a study in every hue of gold: the sun-bleached hair, the delicate blonde eyebrows, those eyes which darkened from topaz to amber, the bronzed skin. Always, after he'd worked for a while, he would extend his palm and brush it lightly over her breasts, then down along her stomach to the dark-blonde hair between her thighs. And then he would make love to her slowly, while her face wore that ardent, helpless look which invariably drove him wild.

One afternoon, gazing down at her, he thought that she resembled a cat, those yellow eyes narrowed against the sun, the high golden cheekbones. Suddenly she seized his hand and pressed it between her legs. He kissed her, and she began to move, languidly at first, then more wantonly, writhing catlike beneath his hand.

He regarded this change in her – her English repose scorched away, her eyes unseeing and full of a wavering light like the centre of some yellow jewel, her body arching – and he himself was ignited. He moved on top of her and she reached down and caressed him with her special touch, and he dragged his tongue up along her body.

It seemed like ages. It was as though he were drowning in her; she was all water and brine. Even through his passion, it occurred to him that, if one were lucky, constancy could be the greatest of love's mysteries, that he could explore her varied selves over and over, that together they could conquer shame. She was at fever pitch; beneath him her body grew tighter and tighter, fighting for its release. And when it came, at that precise moment, just as her wave broke and she began to cry out, he tapped her lightly on the cheek.

He was lying on his back, looking up at the silver-blue sky. "Fleur," he said presently, "Did I–"

"No. I liked it."

He hoisted himself up and studied her, knowing that he would paint her in oils just like this, slumbrous, her face glossed with light and sweat, her hair wheat-pale against the brown skin of her shoulders. She opened her eyes, so golden that they seemed glazed or enamelled with the sunlight, and he marvelled that there was not the merest smudge of green in them. They were a honey-yellow to their depths – would he ever be able to convey that feeling of pure, whorled colour? She smiled, and said, "If the Northern lot would only do *this*, spend their violence in *this* way…"

"There would be peace?" He moved his finger upwards over her breast like a paintbrush.

He thought she might not be serious, but she began to speculate. "I know it's a sixties cliché, 'Make Love Not War', but when two peoples feel so desperately about each other, it can't be only hate, can it? They've been fighting over the same ground for ages, like a badly married couple." She turned her head to look at him. "You know, Tony, I do feel that part of my appeal for you is that I am 'other' – English and Protestant – only you seem able to make good use" (she smiled) "of your fascination. Oh, of course it's another cliché, *odi et amo*, but love *is* the other side of hate, just as you partly resent desiring me. So if they would only reach out towards each other…"

She paused, and he realised that he had never heard her speak of politics at such length and so passionately. How brutal the Troubles were, that they could infect the whole island, moving down from the bitter North to this peaceful garden where they lay.

She went on, "Perhaps it requires some simple gorgeous gesture. Imagine that all the North of Ireland was plunged into darkness, and all their clothes were taken away, and they had to feel for each other under the black sky. Then who would know Protestant from Catholic? They would find only bodies, and maybe sweetness, as they fumbled towards one another, like painters who don't know where they're going but trust to instinct."

• • •

About a fortnight later on another particularly warm day, drowsing on the blanket, idly kissing, they heard a crunch of shoes along the gravel which curved up to the house. They scrambled to their feet, Fleur putting on her dressing gown and

Tony struggling into his jeans but leaving his chest bare. They walked round the corner and saw Gabriel at the door.

Fleur paused, pushing the hair back from her temple. A look of dreamy lovemaking had not yet left her eyes. Tony felt heavy with the heat of the day; he could smell loam, sunlight and sex on his own skin. The intruder smiled at them. "Do come in," said Fleur in her distant English way.

The kitchen was dim to their sun-struck eyes; it seemed to Tony that he and Fleur were stumbling like rabbits as they put the kettle on, smoothed their hair, plucked leaves from their clothes, while Gabriel tilted back in a chair and crossed his legs.

"It occurred to me that you've never seen my work," he said bluntly. "I came to your opening, Tony, and of course everyone knows the paintings of Fleur." He bestowed his charming smile on them. "But, as for myself, I have been labouring in isolation. So I would like to invite you to my house, for a private showing, as it were."

Fleur cleared her throat. "What kind of painting do you do?"

Tony poured out the tea. The skin around his eyes felt taut with apprehension.

Gabriel's smile broadened in a way that Tony could only describe as sinister. He was suddenly aware that this man was terrifically angry, that a nearly ungovernable rage was housed in that smile, that elegant posture, those strong limbs.

Gabriel said, "What kind of painting do I do? Well, lately I have been working on portraits of my parents. They loathe each other, that pair. My mother is a man-hating bitch, and my father is a savage dressed up as a gentleman. I am painting them with blood-red faces and a disgusting substance, like mucus, oozing out of their mouths."

There was a silence. Fleur and Tony looked at each other. Then, "Have a biscuit," suggested Tony, proffering a plate of Fleur's home-made shortbread. He suddenly divined why Gabriel was so much angrier than before, so nearly out of control. He had obviously expected Ballycurry to welcome him with open arms, to extol his genius and generally revere him, but, instead, the opposite was happening. Gabriel was losing his position, even among the easygoing citizens of West Cork. It struck Tony that the man's self-regard had addled his judgement like a fever; he seemed unable to summon forth the tact required of a newcomer. Tony and Fleur had heard that Gabriel was bellicose in the pubs, as though he couldn't comprehend that barroom brawls were alien to this place; that, while the locals might enjoy a kind of teasing banter, they would always recoil from real pugnacity. Slowly, it seemed, the town and the valley were withdrawing from him. Once, when Gabriel walked into Una O'Driscoll's pub, Tony had seen a look of distaste pass over her features before she mustered her habitual welcoming smile.

Closing her dressing gown more firmly, Fleur said tranquilly, "The painting you describe makes me think of Munch's *The Scream*, with that background such a welter of red, like a haemorrhage. And also the macabre paintings of Bosch." She nibbled at a biscuit. "I suppose the challenge, if you're doing that kind of thing, is to avoid merely shocking people. Goya comes to mind, because he is so dark, but full of pathos as well." She paused. "Lately, Tony and I have been fascinated by the North. Because of the ceasefire, people are coming forward, talking about their lives on the evening news; so many stories of woe and brutality, but also of mercy, people's need for mercy, and love, after all that slaughter."

Gabriel gave her a superior smile. "You're saying I shouldn't do violent paintings? That they might *shock* people?"

"There's nothing wrong with a shocking, violent painting, although it might be more interesting if it were informed by other feelings in addition to fury – compassion, perhaps, or rue. That's what I miss in Bacon, although his paintings are terribly powerful."

Tony was trying not to glower at Gabriel, who was obviously impervious to the fact that this woman, an illustrious painter, was favouring him with genuine advice. Scores of acolytes would glow with rapture at the prospect of Fleur Penhalligan discussing their work seriously, and not even in a classroom, but so intimately, over tea, in her own home. Yet this dilettante, lolling like a big tomcat on her kitchen chair, seemed to expect such attention as his due. And his smile was sardonic, practically lascivious. *He knows we've been making love,* Tony thought, *with Fleur in her dressing gown and me bare-chested. He knows, and he's enjoying our discomfiture. And he doesn't really want to talk about the problems of painting; he just wants to be told how good he is.*

Although the kitchen was cool, Tony was aware of the heat outdoors. He longed to be there once again, embracing Fleur in the back garden. He gazed out the open window; bees were blundering against the greenhouse with a soft, thudding sound, and schooners of white cloud were streaming across the sky. *Go away,* he prayed. *Please go away.*

To his astonishment, Fleur said equably, "We shall come tomorrow, in the afternoon, to your studio, if that is acceptable."

Gabriel, bridling, declared yes, yes, tomorrow would be grand, how about four o'clock? Before leaving, he threw Tony a smile – a *gloating* smile, Tony thought.

Fleur began to wash up the tea things. Tony remained at the table, staring at her. He was trembling. "How could you?" he finally managed. "How could you agree to call on that – that monster? And you said '*we*'. I never agreed to go!"

"I didn't want to leave you out," she answered mildly, rinsing the cups.

He drew a shuddering breath. "I don't understand. He comes in here and fouls the air with his arrogance. Don't give me that amused look. He does! Look how he has poisoned this day – *my* day, anyway. And it was you said we shouldn't let people like that get too close–"

"Oh, darling, I shan't let him get close, I promise. It's only that. . ." She returned to the table, extending a hand to him, but he gave her a reproachful look and refused to take it. She went on in a low voice, "I feel nearly abashed when I meet someone who yearns to be an artist but has only a slight gift. My talent, and yours, are accidents, aren't they? We could have been born like him, full of the artist's need to give a shape to things, but unable to. I think we are obliged to be kind to such people. Not *too* kind. I know he would crash through boundaries, if one allowed him to. Not *too* kind, but a *bit*."

Tony said harshly, "How do you know he has no gift? You haven't ever seen his stuff. Perhaps he really is the genius he thinks he is."

She began to push the hair back from her temple with the flat of her hand, in the way which had arrested him when he first saw her. And it continued to move him: such an insignificant gesture, but so utterly her own, and so telling. He wanted to seize that nervous hand now and kiss it into repose, but his anger forbade it.

She said thoughtfully, "It's unlikely that he's a genius, but I suppose it's possible. And if he is gifted, he should be encouraged." She sighed. "I am not intending to befriend him. I shall visit his studio, with or without you, and offer my comments. And that will be that."

"Well, it *will* be without me. You're just guilty, that's all. You feel guilty because you're talented and he isn't, so you've decided to appease the gods by being nice to him. It's all selfish, really. It's all about *you*." His voice was thick with anger. It was not that he didn't sympathise with her, because he did. He had also tried to placate the gods throughout his life, with bargains and prayers, but for now he was fuming – surely she'd gone too far.

"This is all happening in your own head," he persisted. "You might be trying to placate God, but Gabriel doesn't know about that. He's got his own agenda, which has nothing to do with your appeasement policy." He paused, then continued urgently, "Fleur, sometimes those who are most hungry can't be fed, because they're just too damaged! You must try to recognise the difference between compassion and indulging someone's craziness. He'll only take advantage of you – of us." He halted again, wondering where his own hard wisdom had come from; his psychologist father? "And he'll make a play for you," he muttered finally.

She laughed shakily. "I can handle that." Then, "Oh, Tony," she cried, "you have never been a teacher, but *I* have been. It's heartbreaking, the wounded ones, who need so *much*. I promise to keep my distance. I don't *like* him. I am only visiting his studio."

Tony was so appalled at her naivety, he found it impossible to answer. How could she not realise that this Phillips character was a menace? She saw him as needy, which might be true, but there was also the darker side. Didn't she know that there were those who fed on the fame of others, who recognised no distinction between their own ambition and someone else's achievement, who wanted to *become* the famous artist, devour her and take her place? She might feel a desire to comfort the famished, the wounded, from an impulse of guilt or compassion, but couldn't she see that the darkness in Gabriel was real? And did she not care enough for himself, Tony, and for their love, to protect it from such a mad rival?

He was angrier than he'd thought; he found himself shouting, "Don't *patronise* me. Go on and visit his studio, if you must, although the man is probably dangerous. Incidentally, his cheeky girlfriend made a pass at me at the gallery party. She asked me to call on her, to read her poetry. Maybe I'll take her up on it, since, as you say, these wounded birds need our help. Besides, she's closer to my own age."

Tony had always believed in the power of language to illuminate and console; he had never thought much about how words can dirty the truth, and idly hurt. Now the gunsmoke of his words lay between them; for a moment he couldn't breathe. Then Fleur stood up slowly, as though she were in physical pain, and walked over to the basin. She began to wash up the remaining tea things, mechanically rinsing each plate and spoon. Her hair had spilled forward across her cheek, concealing her face from him.

"Fleur—"

"I think you should go home," she said softly, still methodically washing the dishes. "I think you should go back to your own house."

A panic was dinning in his ears. He also stood up, but roughly, so that his chair overturned with a clatter. He had a brief fantasy that Gabriel was crouched at the window, peering in and laughing. "Fleur, forgive me. I didn't mean it. Please."

A few nights before, wakeful for some reason, he had gazed at her asleep beside him on the pillow. The room was flushed with moonlight, in which he could see, clearly, her closed eyes with their toffee-coloured lashes, the slight wrinkles scoring her brow. Gingerly, so as not to rouse her, he had touched the grey which stippled the fair hair at her temples. She would grow old before him. He remembered the Greek myth where a loving couple ask only one favour of the gods, that they should die together; and when the time comes, both are transformed simultaneously into trees, whose boughs interlace, so that they might embrace for eternity. But that would not happen for Fleur and himself. He would know, too early, the decline of his beloved. Her beauty would dim, her vigour would lessen, at a time when he was still robust; she would probably die first, and he would have to live a long time in a world which would seem desolate without her. Gently, he touched her few grey hairs. It didn't matter that she would die before him. None of it mattered. This was his portion; she was the love of his life.

But now, when it was needed, he hadn't the words to say it. She had sealed herself off from him. Observing her while she dried her hands on a tea towel, he wondered could he possibly explain: *The other night, I looked at your grey hair, and I knew I would love you for ever.* Perhaps he *could* speak that very phrase, no matter how awkward it might make him feel in the light of day. Yet, looking at her remote face, the words turned to ash in his mouth. All he could summon was, "Don't send me away."

"I would like to be alone." Then, as though moved by his expression of misery despite herself, she amended, "I would like to be alone, for a while."

He walked down the road in a stoor of anguish. He had known a similar panic as a child, when his father had been harsh and his mother's conciliatory flutterings had merely deepened her son's anxiety. Now, the evening clouds were pewter-coloured, the mountains violet. But nature's beauty could not begin to comfort him.

In his heart of hearts he knew that this was merely their first quarrel. But another voice in his head – the voice which always accompanied his black panics – assured him that he had blown it, had *said the wrong thing*, and now all was lost; she would never forgive him. This voice reminded him of Gabriel; it belonged to Gabriel's world of savagery, of unassuagable hurt, of charnel-house parents, their mouths oozing a putrescence. *Ah*, he said bitterly to himself, *maybe there* is *a bit of Gabriel in us all, which is why Fleur tries to be kind to him.*

•••

He had been returning to his house every day, to work in the room he'd transformed into a studio, but the living quarters – the kitchen and front room and his bedroom – had lain empty since his first night in Fleur's arms. Now they seemed the very embodiment of his new loneliness, those neglected rooms, exhaling a censorious dust.

He decided to write her a letter. *Dear Fleur,* he began, but paused, gnawing the top of his pen. Perhaps "Dear Fleur" was too pallid. *My dearest, darling Fleur.* No, too smarmy. He sighed, thinking of those heroes in old films who cry, "Darling, I've been a fool!" always to good effect, the heroines falling into their arms. *My love, please forgive me for hurting you. I didn't mean. . .*

He went into the kitchen and drank a very large whiskey. Dusk was approaching, and the birds were singing their hearts out. He drank another whiskey, then a third. He was standing, staring fixedly down at his feet, thinking of his vagabond early life, how he had moved from place to place with his temperamental father and phlegmatic mother, how Fleur had become his real home. But now, even the saucepans, the teapot, seemed to be taunting him: *You thought you could escape, but we have dragged you back to loneliness, your rightful position; how could you believe you deserved better?*

When he glanced up and looked sluggishly about him, he was astonished to see that night had fallen. Suddenly, as though an invisible hand were pushing him, he lurched out the door and down along the road.

She had not gone to bed; her windows were lighted. He staggered up to the kitchen door and pounded on it, shouting her name. When she opened it, he stumbled into her arms, so heavily they both nearly toppled to the floor. He clutched at her, pressing his face into her shoulder and groaning, feeling like some lubberly, sweating animal.

"Why, Tony," she exclaimed, "you're drunk!"

"Yes, drunk!" he shouted against her shoulder, sobbing.

"Hush," she murmured. He felt her lips in his hair. "Hush, dear. Let's go to sleep. It's all right."

• • •

But it wasn't all right, or at least not completely. He wanted to tell her about his revelation of just a few nights before, in this very bed, how her greying hair, the fact of her mortality and his own, had brought him to the very heart of his love for her. He suspected that until he told her this, she would doubt him just a bit, fear that he might leave her when she grew old. Foolishly, he had loosed a serpent into their garden, and while he knew it was only a phantom, she was not sure, nor would she be until he explained. Since he was so familiar with her gestures, her soft cries during lovemaking, he could feel, now, a difference, something slightly wooden in her body, even while she was embracing him and soothing him towards sleep. *I must explain*, he said groggily to himself, *and then she will believe in me again.* But at the moment he was too drunk and too dull with relief. It was enough for now that she had taken him back. He would speak to her tomorrow.

And then, and then. . . There was also the other thing. He was still quite angry with her for agreeing to call on Gabriel, still aghast at what he couldn't but consider a caprice. Gabriel was white-hot with rage and dangerously grandiose. In short,

he was a shit, and Tony still couldn't understand why Fleur
would wish to involve herself with him in any way.

Tony realised that he himself was insecure, as well. The
thought of that madman trying to seduce his beloved – which
he would doubtless do – made Tony shake with anger. First of
all, he was afraid for Fleur, since it was clear to him that someone as vain as Gabriel would not swallow rejection happily. But
he was also, very slightly, troubled on his own behalf. Unfortu-
nately Gabriel was very handsome, with those grey eyes and
that patrician carriage, and he was rich as well and about Fleur's
age. Was there a chance she would feel tempted?

Staring at the ceiling, Tony realised that even by entertain-
ing such a fear he was committing an injustice to Fleur and to
their love. But it galled him that she should have rewarded
Gabriel for his impertinence today, that he should have sauntered out of her kitchen feeling triumphant. That smile he'd
thrown at Tony – it was outrageous! Surely such an intruder
should be discouraged, not built up. Oh, he was confident, that
one. He was probably relishing his victory at this very moment,
lying in his bed and smirking, convinced that he had dazzled
Fleur with his style this afternoon and that he would woo her
successfully. Tony moved impatiently on the pillow, dismayed
to acknowledge that he felt obscurely betrayed by her, just as
she was undoubtedly disappointed in him. Tomorrow, he
promised himself, tomorrow we will talk it all out and make it
better.

He gazed through a parting in her curtains at the night sky,
thick with stars. A distant sheep bleated; Fleur, his love, murmured something in a dream. Should he accompany her to

Gabriel's house tomorrow, despite his disapproval, in order to protect her? Maybe. . . Sudddenly weary of thought, he felt himself falling into a murky sleep.

Chapter 8

TOWARDS MORNING TONY dreamt of Rome, of a street where he had lived briefly long ago, when his father was lecturing at an Italian university for a season. In the dream he is gazing out a window at the house opposite, at its blistered ochre walls, listing with age. Its shutters are closed, except for the window directly across from Tony's own. There, a small boy stands, staring back at him, and Tony is struck by how closely the child resembles his former self, how he could very nearly *be* himself as a child: dark, hesitant, skinny, with shy brown eyes. In this dream it is clearly siesta-time. The sun-scorched road is static, empty – the whole city seems caught in a thrall of heat. Tony and the little boy are the only people in Rome who have not lain down to sleep in shuttered rooms. They regard each other, and slowly Tony's heart begins to break. *I love you,* he wants to call out, but before he can utter the words, a hand appears from one side and draws the boy away; Tony hears a faint woman's voice, scolding. Then, abruptly, the shutters close, and it is as though they have closed upon his heart.

His eyes opened. It was very early, barely dawn, and Fleur was still asleep. He got softly out of bed and wove blearily into the toilet, then put on his dressing gown and went down to make a pot of tea. He was buttering a piece of toast when, shockingly, the phone rang. Still half-asleep, he hurried to answer.

"Hello?" His mouth was parched from the whiskies he had drunk the night before, and there was a sour feeling in his stomach.

"Tony?" quavered his mother.

He had not yet fully voyaged back from the land of dreams; that old stone house and the boy's face were still more real to him than his conscious life. So that now, to hear his mother's voice, at dawn, in Fleur's front room, was profoundly eerie, made him literally weak at the knees. He collapsed on to a chair, staring out at the garden. She had to repeat his name three times before he could reply.

"Mother? How did you know – how did you contact me here?"

She reminded him that he had left this number on his answerphone at home. He was preparing himself for an onslaught of motherly inquiries – *Why are you not at Hugh's house? Whose number is this?* – when she told him, "Your father died. Two hours ago. His heart. It was very sudden."

The air began to throb and his heart to fall, turning over and over. How can someone you love vanish from the world?

The conversation proceeded mechanically, emotionlessly.

Tony presumed they were both feeling that to express the raw-
ness of their grief on the telephone would be wrong somehow,
false and awkward. It would wait until he flew to New York,
where his parents had been living since his father retired.

He returned to the bedroom and put his hand on Fleur's
shoulder. She extended her arms and drew him down beside
her; she knew something was wrong, had heard the phone.

He kissed her and caressed her body, not with passion but a
kind of desperate tenderness. "My father died today," he said
dully. Then, thinking aloud, "I must hire a car in the village
and take the first plane I can get. I'll probably only be gone a
few days."

She murmured consolation, smoothing his hair.

"I will miss you," he cried, and was suddenly awash with
guilt, because he did not want to leave her, or his painting, or
this landscape, this world, his life here, which he lived with
such intensity. New York seemed a remote and lonely place, by
comparison, and he could do nothing for his father now. But
he was still sorry, and guilty, that he could muster so little desire
to see his poor mother. He supposed it was because she was
such a strong woman in her unruffled way, had always been
resilient and would certainly be all right now, would go sturdi-
ly on with her life after a period of sorrow, with or without her
son by her side. But he did think he should be more dutiful and
filial, instead of missing Fleur even while she was still cradled
in his arms.

• • •

New York was everything he feared it would be: shrill, hot and
curiously unreal. His father's funeral was discreet, presided over

by a soft-voiced Unitarian minister. (Because Anthony Daly Senior had been a staunch atheist and denouncer of the Catholic church, Tony's mother had considered Unitarianism a tactful compromise, with its progressive attitudes and theological vagueness.)

Longingly, Tony recalled the funerals of Ballycurry, where people did not cordon themselves off from natural processes, but lived close to the source of things, death being simply part of the rhythm. He remembered the funeral of Timothy Donegan, a Ballycurry publican who'd died suddenly the March before of a heart attack, much like Tony's father. The first night, they had crowded into the funeral home for the rosary, Timothy lying encircled by all the villagers who had drunk in his pub, by the shushing of their prayers and the rasp of their beads, like surf dragging over shingle. The second night had been the removal; again that praying crowd, smelling of wool and pipe-smoke, and then the procession to the church under the alert eye of Garda Caffrey, who had saluted Timothy's coffin smartly. The third day, after the funeral, Tony and the others had gone to Timothy's pub where his daughters were serving free drink to all. Everyone had toasted dead Timothy with sorrow, but also the strange exhilaration, the passion for life which funerals enkindle in people, compelling them to drink and eat with a grateful fervour.

How unsatisfying his father's funeral seemed in comparison, how cold and stilted. There was a brief service in the antiseptic funeral home. Then the pastor (with a coyly pious downward look) placed the urn of ashes into his mother's hands. After that, Tony and Mrs Daly and a very few guests repaired to her

Greenwich Village apartment for a drink and a cold meal provided by the local deli.

When, after a polite length of time, the guests had all gone, Tony looked exhaustedly around at the remains of the funeral feast: whiskey and wine and plates of baked meat. "Let's clean up," his mother suggested. "I need to be doing things."

While they were ferrying plates and glasses into the kitchen, she said, "Tony, where were you when I called? Have you a new girlfriend?"

He hesitated. "Yes. It's pretty serious. She's a painter, too."

"Oh? That's nice," answered his mother meaninglessly, her eyes bright. She was clearly trying to restrain herself, but he could feel her eagerness to pelt him with questions.

He said cautiously, "Her name is Fleur. Fleur Penhalligan. You've heard of her? No? Well, I suppose she wouldn't be that well-known outside the painting world. Within it, though, she has quite a reputation."

A pause. Then the inevitable, dreaded question. "A reputation? How old is this gir– woman?"

He was putting a bottle of half-drunk white wine back into the fridge. "Oh, fortyish," he replied casually, his back to her.

She was silent a while, wrapping up the leftovers. Tony realised that his eyes were burning; he was so bleary from the time-change and so depleted with grief he felt haggard, in need of a bath, as though his tiredness were a layer of dirt on the skin.

His mother said, "Fortyish? Why, that's only about ten years younger than me!"

He didn't want to be having this conversation. To make light of it, he cried, "Well, Mother, no doubt Dad would say I'm at the mercy of the good old Oedipus Complex, once again. It's really *you* I desire." He made to playfully embrace her, but she moved away.

"Tony, why is this older woman interested in you? What designs has she on you?"

He registered, with some bitterness, that she didn't seem concerned as to why her young son was interested in the "older woman". Part of the source of his present-day shyness was this attitude of his mother. She had never wondered, in the classic maternal way, was so-and-so good enough for Tony, but only if they liked *him*, and why. Normally a phlegmatic woman, she had become anxious only when Tony brought friends home or described his teachers to her, after which she would invariably ask, "Did you conduct yourself well? Were they pleased with you?" her eyes wide with worry. Nor had he welcomed her support when his father scolded him; she had seemed too anxious at those times also, full of an unseemly pity for him.

Now, he tried not to sound exasperated. "That's a strange question. You might have thought that I would be the one with designs. After all, she's a famous painter and I'm just a novice. I could be trying to exploit her for my own career. What designs would she possibly have on me?"

His mother was bunching a tea towel in her hands. "Well, you are young and . . . strong."

He gave a rather shrill laugh, which alarmed him. He supposed he must be dangerously near hysteria from all the emotions of the past few days, to say nothing of the transatlantic flight. "Oh, Mother, are you thinking that she covets me because of my youthful virility? That she wants to *use me up* in some sordid, *sexual* way?" Again he laughed too raucously; then took a deep breath, fighting to control himself. "Oh, Mother," he repeated finally, as steadily as he could, "please don't worry. I truly love Fleur. Of course I'd prefer it if she were younger, since it would give us more time together. But she is what she is. People's psyches and spirits are ageless, I think. Anyway, we really get along, Fleur and I, and the age thing doesn't bother us. Or it hasn't so far, and I'm pretty positive about the future."

She muttered something about grandchildren.

"Fleur isn't *that* old," he rebuked her, but hesitated: when *did* women go through the menopause? "Anyway," he concluded, "we are happy."

"Then I am happy for you," said his mother, with an apprehensive smile.

• • •

Over the next few days he took to walking through New York. He liked where his mother lived, deep in the West Village, full of leafy, dreamy streets, and then by the river, full of a sheer sea light, which shone with a salty radiance on the romantically dilapidated bars (labourers' bars and gay bars) and the *chic* cafés.

He also walked uptown, to visit the Metropolitan Museum of Art, the Modern and the Guggenheim. What a great city, after all, but how exhausting. At one point, walking along the lozenged footpath of Central Park, at the border of Fifth Avenue, his feet aching from hours of picture-gazing, he considered going into one of the hotels across the street to rest and have a drink.

Too expensive, he decided ruefully, taking in the solemnly opulent facades of the Pierre and Sherry Netherland, with their liveried doormen. He suddenly remembered that this was where Gabriel had come from; he had lived here, on Fifth Avenue, perhaps in that building on the corner, a dark fortress, its windows glinting almost ominously, as though to say Keep Out to the likes of himself.

Slowly, he turned around and began to walk back the way he had come, uptown towards the museums. And while he walked he stared across Fifth Avenue at the houses of the rich, at their stern grandeur, their canopies, their doormen, wearing silly white gloves despite the summer heat, helping ladies out of taxis, carrying their shopping bags into cool foyers.

One might suppose that Gabriel would have no right to be as mentally troubled as he was, coming from such a life as this, such extraordinary privilege. But Tony was divining something, feeling something, as he looked at the houses along Fifth Avenue. At one window a girl appeared, shadowy behind the thick glass; he could just make out her aureole of red hair and grey maid's uniform. She seemed almost a prisoner. She appeared to be gazing at Central Park before turning abruptly back into her fishbowl.

Tony tried to remember what the Ballycurry gossips had told him about Gabriel's background. (Ballycurry, so far away, was still as vivid to him as anonymous New York.) Was Gabriel's father a robber baron, a captain of industry? No, a lawyer, Tony recalled, some kind of ruthless society lawyer. He continued to reflect, conjuring up Gabriel's arrogant face, and was suddenly struck by something: the poor man feared that he did not exist!

Tony stopped in the middle of the path; a woman, trundling a pram, manoeuvred past him with an annoyed look. It had suddenly become clear; Gabriel had finally come into focus. And for the first time since they had met, Tony could feel compassion for him. *Gabriel fears that he is not real, fears that he is an invisible man.*

In one of those sombre piles, behind just such formidable windows, Gabriel had been made to feel small. No, worse than small. He, Tony, had felt small whenever his mother had fluttered about him with her anxious queries, *Do they like you? Did you please them? Did you make your dad angry?* No, something worse, much worse, must have happened to Gabriel. His desire for attention, fame, was no ordinary ambition. What had they done to him to make him feel so helpless, a pebble falling through empty air? Obviously, as a child, his cries had gone unanswered. Surely all children cry out in the night, thought Tony, since their world is peopled with monsters, as well as angels. But clearly Gabriel's fears were never assuaged; no loving Proustian mother, caressing his forehead, had assured him that she would protect him from the ogres who thronged his dreams, no proud father had made him feel armoured in love. Gabriel had painted them as ghouls: *My mother is a man-hating bitch, and my father is a savage dressed up as a gentleman.* He had never been favoured in their sight; he was terrified still.

Tony continued to trudge uptown, ignoring his fatigue. He had phoned Fleur a few days before. Describing her visit to Gabriel's studio, she had said, with a sigh, that the work was not focused: "He's all over the place, Tony. Some of the paintings are sub-Delaunay, some rather derivative of Bridget Riley,

some utterly abstract but not thought-out, and others are merely grotesque. He has studied everything and achieved nothing."
She had paused before continuing, "But, you know, it's curious, there is something which is compelling in the work. One
senses that he does have talent, only it's been strangled or sti-
fled. He tried to tell me about a desire of his to paint a kind of
green source in his life, *something* to do with nature, but I was
too distracted to listen properly. Anyway, I doubt if he could
make the journey into himself that art demands. . . I do think
that beneath his arrogance he feels terribly insecure. It was quite
awkward."

"I will see you in a few days," Tony had replied, "It *must* have
been awkward. Poor Fleur." But now, at last, he was also able
to think, *Poor Gabriel; poor wretched man, unable to channel his
hurt.*

He plunged east, to Madison Avenue, where a coffee shop
caught his eye. He went in, thinking, This *is New York*: the
burly cook brandishing a spatula beside the open, sizzling grill;
the counter where cakes and pies were displayed under plastic
covers, and where strangers, comfortably side-by-side, were eating plates of food and drinking coffee from thick white cups.
The bustle, the door which jingled when opened, the calls of
the waitresses, the formica tables, the throb of the air condi-
tioner were like something in a film, but they were real; New
York was really like this.

He settled at the counter, imagining that Fleur was beside
him, savouring this place with him. Suddenly he missed her
with such force it was like a fist in his stomach. He still hadn't
told her about the depth of his love, assured her that he would

not forsake her over time. His hands on the menu began to
tremble, as though his yearning were making him physically
sick; he forced himself to concentrate on the daunting array of
dishes. He could have moussaka, spaghetti bolognese, *salade
Niçoise*, an omelette, baked cod, Yankee pot roast. He decided
on a turkey sandwich (white, rye, whole wheat, a roll or a bagel?
asked the waitress) and a glass of milk (low-fat or whole?).

The place was pleasantly cool and growing more drowsy as
the lunch hour passed. Before leaving, the man beside Tony
offered him his *New York Times*.

Tony ordered a coffee (regular, decaf, espresso or cappucci-
no?) and leafed through the paper. A longish article arrested
him, a story about a young man, his own age, who had been
convicted of a murder in Alabama. It was his grandfather he
had killed, a brutish old man by all accounts. Neighbours had
testified that he beat his grandson regularly, often until the
child lost consciousness, and there was evidence of sexual abuse,
as well. But the grandfather's life had also been hard. He had
been born sub-normal, or, according to the euphemistic *New
York Times*, "mildly mentally disabled", at a time when there
were no special schools or therapists to minister to such children, or at least not in rural Alabama. His parents, abashed and
finally angered by his inability to learn, had put him into foster care, and so he'd gone from orphanage to foster home and
back again, until at some point he married a local girl as afflicted as himself. They had a daughter who died, leaving them
with her newborn boy. Then the wife had also died.

Tony read on, wondering why this story absorbed him so.
The grandson had grown up in squalour, at the mercy of the

old man who was a terror in the community, shouting at shopkeepers, threatening callers with a rifle. His house stank of unwashed linen and rancid grease. Clergymen and school-teachers, recognising that he was growing more and more deranged, tried to advocate on his grandson's behalf, but the local court decreed that old Mr Renfrew had every right to care for his daughter's child; they were each other's only blood relations, after all. Anyway, it seemed the whole town simply wanted shut of it. That family were just too sordid and embarrassing.

After the trial, a controversy ensued as to whether the young man should be put to death. A few lonely voices cried out in defence of him: his high school history teacher, a nurse who had bandaged him after one of the grandfather's frenzies, the foreman at a factory where he'd worked briefly. But the consensus was that he should die. The *New York Times* had interviewed various townspeople, who spoke, Tony thought, with a heartless satisfaction about the boy "learning his lesson" about eyes for eyes and teeth for teeth. "Fry him," declared one of his neighbours. "Let him reap what he sowed." Tony considered this one of the most appalling mixed metaphors he had ever encountered.

Moral rectitude, vengeance, blood sacrifice; how long would they insist that our wounded world could be cleansed with blood? Tony lowered the paper. Something was happening to him. It had begun when he pondered Gabriel today, but it hadn't stopped there. It was growing within him, struggling to be born, and like most of his mental journeys, it took the form of an incipient painting.

He pictured Glenfern at dawn, when those membranous webs, pearled with dew, were draped like bridal finery from branch to branch along the hedge. Dawn was a particularly secret time in Glenfern, the hedges filmed with that starry gauze, birds bursting from it with sharp cries.

Next he thought of the web of his own body, filaments of vein, lattices of bone, cables of sinew and tendon, the crackling synapses of the brain. And then he considered the web of the world, the story of our humanity, in which we are, each one of us, implicated. The evil grandfather as a gibbering boy, forsaken by his parents, growing up like a beast; his cowed grandson, also forsaken, exploding finally into murderous anger. The dark side, the dark side. His own sex fantasies about Fleur, how her soft helpless cries made him want to hurt her, ravish her. His fear of Gabriel. Gabriel himself, broken, probably anguished, unable to love or mourn the father and mother he'd never really had, marooned in a cold universe.

Remembering his own father, Tony suddenly began to cry, silently, concealing his face behind the newspaper. Today was Wednesday. He couldn't wait for Friday, when he would fly back to Ireland and to Fleur, homewards.

Chapter 9

THE DAY FLEUR was to visit him, Gabriel dismissed Lottie early. She was standing by the window in a panel of sunlight, so that he could barely make out her shape.

"Lottie, move away from the window. I can't see you in all that light."

Sullenly, she walked towards him, into the relative dimness of the room. Today her hair was bound up with a bandana, improvised from a red scarf. A green cloth was clutched in her hand; she'd been dusting the books. She looked exceptionally pretty. He stared over her shoulder.

"Lottie, please go home early today." He hadn't meant to be so brusque, but the circumstances were awkward. How could he tell her that he wanted to be alone for Fleur's visit? He was hoping that she would come without Tony, and the last thing he needed was a vexatious Lottie trudging through the house while he was trying to talk seriously with a fellow artist.

She gave him one of her sharp looks. "Why?"

He sighed. "It isn't really your concern, is it? I just happen to be in need of some privacy. For my work." *Damn her*, he was thinking. He'd always considered himself a talented dissembler, but this girl had an almost uncanny radar, an instinct for divining his lies and ferreting out his real motives which invariably threw him off balance.

She dragged the bandana off, shook out her curls and threw the green cloth on the floor. "Grand. I'll clear off, then. There's a *tiny* lasagna in the oven. Enough for *one.*" She made to flounce away, but paused at the door. "Don't think I don't know," she said slowly, almost tauntingly. "Don't think I don't know why you're throwing me out." She narrowed her eyes in that feral way of hers. "You're such a bastard, Gabriel. You don't even realise when someone is giving you something. When someone *knows* you and still – wants to care about you. . ."

He looked at her in astonishment. Why, it seemed that she was trying to tell him that she *loved* him. He nearly burst out laughing. What a manipulative bitch! He supposed he was meant to feel chagrined now. If this were a film, he would cry, "Darling, I had no idea!" while music surged behind and they collapsed into each other's arms. As it was, she would cycle home now feeling dignified and ill-used, pleased that she had put him in his place. She loved him about as much as he loved her, the little cynic.

"Very good, Lottie," he answered with a laugh; "I'm glad you care for me. You're a fine girl yourself. Now be good and go home. And don't worry. I'll pay you for the whole day."

So much for her guile, he thought triumphantly. He was glad to make it plain that she had not deceived him with her spurious love talk. Over the years he had schooled himself never to rely on people. How dare she use the currency of love, traffic in its expressions? He was pleased to remind her of the real basis of their relationship: she needed him for money, and he liked her for sex.

Before leaving she gave him a look of pure loathing, which he ignored. And after she'd clambered on to her little bicycle and disappeared in the direction of Ballycurry, he amusedly pictured her pedalling home, those sky-blue eyes staring angrily at the road ahead.

But when he turned back, his amusement vanished, to be replaced by an unsettled feeling. They *were* so blue, her eyes. He'd got used to them and to having her around. The place felt different without her, empty. And it struck him that the red scarf and green cloth she had discarded on the floor looked curiously pathetic, like two forsaken toys. This thought alarmed him, since he was not usually so fanciful.

Muttering to himself, he went into the kitchen to make a coffee, something Lottie would ordinarily have done for him. His own was wan in comparison, he acknowledged with a grimace. It was occurring to him, as he emptied his unfinished cup into the basin, that he might indeed have disdained a real gift, that her surliness might after all conceal a genuine affection for him, yet he had laughed at her.

And once more he observed that the two of them were alike; they were both afraid. But of what? He had wandered up to his studio and was gazing at one of his more recent abstracts, all rich colour – red, gold and orange – done in misty panels; almost like a Rothko. The question persisted: *Afraid of what?*

An answer seemed to float up from some unrealised source in his own unconscious.

He feared that a monster dwelt in the warrens of his psyche, a kind of Grendel blundering through an arid thicket, the very opposite of his "green" vision. He had hated his parents, had wanted to kill them. And now he was afraid that if anyone looked into his secret self, if they looked and saw the sulphurous fury there, they would die of it, literally die of the shock. Was this the reason he could not paint certain visions, even the ones closest to his heart? With a sudden, irritable gesture, he walked out of the room, determined to banish any troublesome thoughts. Today would be important, and he must not fuck it up with glum reflections, or compunctions about Lottie, who was after all just a silly girl and unable to help him, as Fleur Penhalligan might do.

• • •

Fleur arrived precisely at four o'clock. He gestured her into the kitchen. He had got over his earlier gloom and was jubilant that she'd come alone. "Would you like a cup of tea?"

"That would be nice," she said vaguely. He had noticed immediately that she was distracted.

"Are you troubled about something?" he asked, trying to sound solicitous rather than peevish.

She seemed to have difficulty focusing on him. "Yes, I am. Sorry. You see, Tony had to leave abruptly this morning, to drive to Cork and get a plane for America. His father died suddenly. I'm terribly worried about him."

Gabriel felt a glow of delight that Tony was out of the picture, at least for a while. "Oh, dear. Can I do anything to take your mind off it? Would you like to go out to dinner? Fiona's has marvellous–"

As at the Ballybracken gallery, her eyes darkened suddenly, deepening from their usual honey colour to a russet brown. "No, thank you. Tony may ring tonight, and I should like to be at home for his call."

Gabriel accepted this; it was good enough that he had her to himself now. Almost shyly, because he so seldom spoke about these things, he began to describe his secret obsession, how he had always cherished the Irish countryside. "As a child it sustained me," he said with a slightly abashed smile, "this romance with nature. Only I can't get it into my work. Or not directly. I do paint light often, sheer light like Delaunay, and that might have something to do with the light of Ireland, how it impressed itself on my imagination when I was small. But I can't paint landscapes. I mean, who can these days, without being trite? If I tried, it would look like 'The Peaceable Kingdom' or something. It would trivialise what I had felt, a kind of wistful feeling I suppose, when I did actually spend days and days wandering through the fields."

He stopped, sensing an impatience in her. Although she was drinking her tea dutifully, she kept fiddling with her spoon and glancing over his shoulder. Once again, he had to suppress annoyance. He had been honouring her with confidences he had never vouchsafed anyone, yet she was not listening. And yesterday he'd driven all the way to the gourmet food shop in Schull to buy the makings of a Cornish tea for her, but now, here she was, eating her scone listlessly, barely noticing the home-made jam and clotted cream. Would Tony Daly intrude on this day, become a presence in this house, even while he was flying across the Atlantic? Gabriel nearly rebuked her, but restrained himself. She was too important for his career; he must harness his temper. Anyway, perhaps she was simply eager to see his paintings, especially since the light was so fine today. He put down his cup and suggested they go to the studio.

While she moved slowly from canvas to canvas, he regarded her. She was wearing one of her floaty dresses, with blue sandals; her hair gleamed in the light from the window. Her face was so intent. He felt a tremor of hope.

Presently she said, "You are trying different styles, I see. It's intriguing to observe your work process." She paused, pushing at her hair with the flat of her hand. "But surely, at this point, you should be developing your own style. If you would like to flourish as an artist. . ." Again she paused. The canvases seemed to be holding their breath. "If you would like to flourish as an artist, the work must *speak*. In its own voice, if you see what I mean. It's not about the artist asserting his uniqueness through technical display. The work must speak for itself, which requires focus and discipline. And the artist must be humble. After all, he or she is only a conduit, through which the vision flows."

Anticipating homage, he had begun to smile. And after she had spoken the smile remained on his face, as in that New York restaurant long ago, when his father had wounded him. He looked silently at her, and the familiar anger blazed through him, a white incandescence. But he continued to smile.

She went on, "I don't feel *you*, your vision, in these paintings. Not yet. They seem to be experiments, warm-up exercises."

He still hadn't quite absorbed the fact that she was putting him down. When it finally registered, his rage deepened, flared like a sore tooth. He had let her see his work, and now she was trying to reduce him to *nothing*. Suddenly he remembered a time when he was small and his father was reviling him once again, in yet another restaurant, and he had wet himself.

He said slowly, "You are telling me my paintings are not good." But what he was picturing in his head was that scene in the restaurant: his father's bright cruel voice, his own face aching with the effort to keep smiling, the tears just behind his eyes; and then, shockingly, something much worse than tears, that disgusting flow down his leg. Instantly, protectively, he reversed the picture and saw this woman at his mercy, himself violating her; how he would exult to see her splayed beneath him! She would like it – all these prim English girls liked rough sex. It might even improve *her* art.

"No," she answered hastily, "I'm not saying that at all. You may have a considerable gift, but it's still undeveloped. Perhaps you have been too impatient, Gabriel, too eager to break through. It doesn't happen quickly, for most of us. I should know, because it took me years. One must work on and on, until the painting comes alive. Certainly, I understand the desire for recognition. No one wants to paint in a vacuum. But it *does* take time. If I were you, I should keep to one vision, one challenge." She gestured towards a particular canvas. "I'm interested in that picture of the New York fire escapes. You've made them look so intricate and *bony* against the walls, like external skeletons. New York seems to be one of your principal

landscapes. Oughtn't you to pursue it? It would make an interesting contrast with West Cork."

He could barely speak, remembering how she had not listened when he had tried to describe his struggle to realise the
very vision she was now disdaining. The anger was a beating of
wings in his head; through it he was becoming aware that, no
matter how much charm he might switch on, she would
remain impervious to him. His good looks, his talent, had not
ruffled her glacial English composure. He'd been sure that if he
could only see her alone he would be able to impress her, but
now he knew with a bitter certainty that neither his paintings
nor he himself would ever move her.

In a dim way he also knew that the things she was saying
were true. He had never really attempted to paint what his
heart commanded. He was forced to acknowledge that she
could not, after all, address his green vision, since he had not
yet brought it on to canvas. He did understand that it was not
enough for an artist to have a rich interior life if it stayed
inchoate, but he had always believed that he would naturally
become a true artist once the world acknowledged his special-
ness. It was as though he stumbled through meagre spaces,
aware that deeper rooms existed in the house of the spirit, but
unable to find them. He had observed other people closely, and
thought he knew how to charm them, but they were not alto-
gether real to him. He was desperately afraid of failure and deri-
sion, and it seemed to him that these things were embodied
now in Fleur, in her cautious comments and tolerant smile.

And remembering how he had dismissed Lottie that morning, a fresh rage surged in him. Poor Lottie, sacrificed for this

frigid bitch, cycling home broken-hearted. And he knew her well enough to predict that at this point she would force him to plead and apologise for days before agreeing to come back. Anyway, thanks to Fleur, he would have no woman today.

She was still talking, but he could hear her only dimly through the rushing in his head. Somehow they had got down to the kitchen, and she had put her hand on the door, was about to leave. He realised that he was still smiling. Suddenly, without thinking, he extended his hand and grasped her arm.

She gave him a level look. An internal voice, shearing through his fury, told him he must not hurt this woman. She was too assured; she was not afraid of him as Ardyth had been. And besides, she might yet help him. He said thickly, "I thought – I thought you might like a drink."

"No, thank you." When he still did not release her, she said calmly, "Let go my arm, Gabriel."

He dropped his hand, and without another word, she walked out.

• • •

Then followed the days of his penance, when Lottie would not speak to him. The weather also changed abruptly. In the mornings the sky was an ominous oyster colour, a glaucous white and grey, and thick with crows spiralling high into the air, like bits of charred paper caught in a wind. Each afternoon the rain began, falling steadily, while the temperature remained uncomfortably warm. Now and again, the rain eased and a bleary white sun appeared behind the clouds, and then the midges would swarm into his garden, eating at him unmercifully if he dared venture out.

Dust gathered in his house, and the bathroom began to smell of mildewed towels. Without Lottie to cook for him, he ate only bread and cheese and the scones he'd bought for Fleur. He took to gin, guzzling it straight from the bottle. And then, on Wednesday afternoon, Farmer Coughlan called with a bottle of poteen concealed under his coat, which Gabriel bought for a fiver. It was like drinking petrol, but by God it did the trick.

Fleur's visit was congealing in him into something foul. Alone in his remote house, its windows cowled with rain, he walked from room to room, thinking about the outlandish things she had said. *How dare she?* was the refrain in his mind, *How dare she?* while he drank poteen and stared at his paintings, which she had wanted to defile. Once, half-drunk and fuming, he glanced into the mirror and saw that his eyes were the same leaden colour as the sky.

Thursday, the weather improved, became dry and bright once again. The air flowered with birdsong. He decided to appeal to Lottie, for about the thousandth time, only in person for a change.

Driving into Ballycurry that afternoon, he thought perhaps he should have collected a bouquet from the garden, to sweeten her. But then he considered how it would look to the busybodies of the village, scrutinising him from behind their lace curtains, if they saw him trudging sheepishly along the high street to Lottie's door, clutching flowers.

His hands on the wheel trembled, and he could sense that his breath was acrid. During the days of bad weather, he had drunk a whole bottle of gin and nearly half the poteen; even that afternoon he'd poured a bit into his coffee, for Dutch courage, he supposed. Now, in the sunshine, he felt begrimed, and promised himself to stop drinking and get back to work: to hell with Fleur Penhalligan.

"You look terrible," said Lottie helpfully, after she'd reluctantly opened the door.

"Thanks. Can I come in?"

She stared at him with her customary inscrutable expression. "No. Fuck off. I'm not coming back."

"Lottie, please let me in. And of course you must come back. How will you make a living?"

"Haven't you ever heard of the *dole*? I suppose you've lived in such a gilded cocoon all your life, you never even knew the dole existed."

He liked that phrase "gilded cocoon". It occurred to him for the first time that she might have some writing talent, after all.

She went on in a low voice, "I know why you sent me away, you absolute bastard. It was to meet Fleur Penhalligan, wasn't it? I saw you walking in the direction of her house the day before, and sure I noticed all kinds of *lovely* things to eat in the fridge."

He laughed. "You're one to talk! Coming on to Tony Daly, and while I was standing right beside you."

She seemed to hesitate, then cried, "Don't you understand anything, you total eejit? I was only. . ." She looked down at her feet, then up at him again, her eyes narrowed. "Don't you understand? I was trying to make you *jealous*." She gave a rather bleak laugh. "And it worked. You *did* get jealous."

He regarded her suspiciously, deciding that her smile and that sere little laugh were meant to be triumphant. She was *laughing* at him. And he was indeed degrading himself for her, petitioning her like a humble suitor, imploring her to let him into her squalid flat. Damn her to hell!

"You think I would ever be jealous about you, Lottie?" he asked with icy incredulity. "*You?* You're just a dirty, stupid, culchie whore."

He dragged each epithet out, lingering over it. He was pleased to be able to use *culchie*, which he'd learned only a few weeks before, when he'd overheard some friendly teasing one evening at O'Driscoll's pub.

Her face went white. He'd actually never seen anybody go pale like that. It was something one read about in books, people's faces blanching with emotion. But now it happened to Lottie; her face turned utterly white and her eyes darkened to an inky violet. In a trembling voice, she said, "I hate you. I've never hated anyone in my life as much as I hate you. If you ever try to speak to me again, I'll – I'll *kill* you." And she closed the door softly in his face.

He waited, aware that he'd made a mistake, wondering what to do. He could hear her crying. He tried calling out her name, but she refused to answer. Finally he pushed at the door and was surprised when it swung open.

She was lying face down on the bed, crying in gulps, as children do when they abandon themselves to misery.

"Come on, Lottie." He settled gingerly beside her, but she only lifted her tear-blotched face for an instant to cry, "Go away!"

Yet when he rolled her over she said nothing. He inserted a hand under her jumper and touched her breasts. She gave a kind of weak wriggle, as if in protest, but then lay still, looking up at him through tears and a tangle of curls.

He dragged off her clothes, and once again she did not resist, but her limbs were wooden. When he removed her jeans and knickers, one leg, then the other, fell heavily back on to the bed. He pushed her thighs apart and caressed her groin; he could feel her excitement, but her body was still stubborn; she would not move for him. He turned her on to her stomach and fucked her in that position while she remained inert, although he knew she came.

He dismounted and got dressed. Neither of them spoke. At the door he said, "So, you'll be coming back, after all?"

From the bed, she stared at him, and he was struck by how like a child she looked, that round face and curly hair. She could have been six years old.

"No, I won't be coming back," she answered slowly.

"Yes, you will." He laughed, and sauntered out into the warm day.

• • •

It was not her generous body but those doll's eyes and apple cheeks, glinting with tears, which continued to haunt him as he walked into the pub. He distractedly asked Nora for a whiskey, before gradually detecting an atmosphere of gloom: some local men and women, along with the ordinarily sanguine Aubrey Bellowes, were staring morosely at a sheet of paper on the bar. Even Nora looked glum.

Whiskey in hand, Gabriel approached the group. A florid farmer-type was saying, "I never thought I'd see the like. A disgrace it is. A disgrace for Ballycurry, which is the cleanest friendliest village in Ireland. And I do know it, for I was quite a traveller in my time."

"So you were, Tommy," cried another rustic-looking man, younger, with tousled hair. "I remember the day you went above to Cork to find a wife and came home with a transistor radio instead." A woman gave this man an admonitory thump on the arm, but they all smiled, even the florid farmer, before scowling down at the paper once again.

Over Aubrey's shoulder, Gabriel read:

TIDY TOWNS COMPETITION OF REP. OF IRELAND

Report on Ballycurry, West Cork

1. Crumpled cigarette packet found in flower box at entrance of Keating's pub.
2. One bag containing two and a half crushed chips and a bit of fried cod found on footpath in vicinity of local takeaway.
3. Canine excrement (two pieces) discovered beside the Allied Irish Bank.
4. Page 4 of the *Cork Examiner* found in gutter beside the outdoor Gents Lavatory of O'Driscoll's pub.

CONCLUSION: Ballycurry is a charming West Cork village. While it does not overlook the ocean, it borders an estuary and greensward with a children's playground. The house fronts are painted bright green, red, blue, etc., in the West Cork tradition, with flower boxes decorating many windows. The committee found the road generally clean and tidy, with the significant exceptions detailed above. In keeping with these four violations of tidiness, we have regretfully decided not to bestow a Tidy Towns Award on Ballycurry.

Gabriel said, "Dog shit beside the *bank*? There's no bank in Ballycurry. That house is just an empty husk now, isn't it?"

Aubrey smiled. "Indeed. But the sign 'Allied Irish Bank' was never removed, which gives the place *gravitas*, I suppose, and bestows symbolic meaning on those dog faeces."

A young woman wearing a mackintosh and wellingtons spoke next – in an English accent. Gabriel realised that, of course, she was not a local at all, but one of the vagabond Brits who were turning acres of West Cork into organic farms and gardens. Earlier he had been inclined to dismiss all such idealistic ex-pats as superannuated hippies, until he'd realised that the love they harboured for Ireland's green places was similar to his own dream.

The woman was repeating, "It simply isn't fair. When you look at other towns, at the rubbish scatttered round the fish and chips shops, it seems awful that they should penalise us for one silly bag in the road with two and a half chips in it. And fags as well. In other towns one sees gutters full of cigarettes, especially after a late night at the pubs. I think that we ought to register some kind of official protest, don't you?" She looked appealingly at them.

Gabriel was beginning to feel galvanised. These villagers, even the polished Mr Bellowes, would not know the ropes as well as a New Yorker like himself. He could direct them all in a real campaign. Under his guidance they would muster all kinds of attention from the media and the government. He pictured television cameras, microphones, himself declaring victory, the Tidy Towners contrite, the Ballycurrians jubilant, then an appearance on the *Late Late Show*, with the discussion swerving from Tidy Towns to his own paintings…

"Of course we should protest," he cried. "And I know just how to go about it. It's no good writing to the Tidy Towns people. They're just moronic lackeys. We've got to go to the top, right away. Radio, TV, the national press."

The red-faced man mumbled, "Well, I suppose we could write letters to *The Southern Star*."

"That's just the *local* press." Gabriel tried not to sound scornful. "I mean *The Irish Times*, and also the *Independent*, both the daily and Sunday editions."

"What about the *Examiner*?" frowned the tousle-haired man, obviously indignant at the notion that their own Cork paper should be slighted. "The people at the *Examiner* would listen to us, sure."

"You're not thinking big enough," Gabriel answered impatiently. "We must think national. We must expose the Tidy Towns Organisation as corrupt and ineffectual. We've got to shame them into submission." He thumped his fist on the bar, causing Nora, who had been drying pint glasses, to turn round for a second. "Sorry," Gabriel muttered.

Aubrey looked at him with a kind of mild sympathy, and also something else that Gabriel could not read. He said gently, "Dear boy, I am sure that the Tidy Towns lot are not corrupt, only a bit too meticulous. They cannot see the forest for the trees, or the village for the fish and chips papers, in this instance. Unfortunate, but not, after all, earth-shattering."

Baffled, Gabriel replied, "But it *is* earth-shattering. For Ballycurry, I mean, for our economy. If we had got a Tidy Towns prize, it would have brought in more tourists, more business. It *is* a disgrace." He swept his eyes over the group, expecting them to cry out in agreement, but a silence had fallen. The English-woman said, "I suppose I shall write a tactful letter to the Tidy Towns Committee, as I suggest we all do. Strength in numbers, you know. Anyway, I must be off."

She murmured a vague goodbye before bustling out, and, as if it were a signal, the tousle-haired farmer and his wife put their empty glasses on the bar and left as well. To those who remained, the rubicund man and Aubrey, Gabriel entreated, "She's totally wrong. Don't you see? It's no use being *tactful*. We've got to be aggressive, or we'll never cow them." He wanted to rekindle the anger he had felt in these people only moments before. It had exhilarated him, made him feel like a crusader fighting for the part of the world he had chosen. But now even the farmer with the flushed face was looking more dismayed than angry, and Aubrey was composedly smoking his pipe and gazing into the middle distance.

The farmer said hesitantly, "You may be right, boyeen, but I am too old to think big. Sure I'll think small, and write a letter to *The Southern Star*. Thanks, Nora." And he also walked out.

Gabriel sighed with frustration. The room had resumed its customary, somnolent afternoon air, with Nora standing at a corner of the bar, pencil poised, intent on a crossword puzzle, and Aubrey continuing to smoke placidly. The brown curtains were caught in a blur of sunlight; a fly hovered above their heads. Presently, Aubrey gave him another sympathetic look. He seemed to pause; then offered, "Your energy is admirable, young man. Perhaps we village folk are merely too unworldly, or lazy, to answer your call to action. Do try not to be too dis-appointed in us."

This pleased Gabriel. The distinguished Aubrey Bellowes actually admired him. It didn't matter that the others had bolted; Aubrey, by far the best of them, had been quietly impressed all along. He nearly called for a second whiskey, and another *digestif* for Aubrey, but remembered, just in time, that he had promised himself to stop drinking and return to work. And with another sigh of relief, he also remembered how he had subdued Lottie today. She would return to him now, he was certain of it; his reading of their situation had been so masterly.

Chapter 10

TONY'S MOTHER ACCOMPANIED him in the taxi to the airport, to prolong their time together. Moving sluggishly through the streets, they gazed out at summertime New York: cars roasting in heavy traffic, office workers crumpling at the bus stops, the sky dulled with humidity and pollution, the East River an exhausted grey-brown.

"You ought to get out of the city, Mother," he suggested. "Go somewhere for a holiday. Come visit me in Ireland." He only half-meant the last proposal.

She seemed to divine his ambivalence, for she squeezed his hand and answered, "You need to be alone, my dear, to paint, and to develop this new . . . relationship of yours." She went on to assure him that she liked New York in the summer; there were concerts in Central Park, open-air plays and beaches nearby. Also, she reminded him that many of her friends and some relatives lived there. She would miss her son but was determined to fashion a new life for herself.

He kissed her, moved by her courage, and guiltily relieved.

• • •

In the thronged terminal, he finally gave himself over to the excitement of returning to Ireland and seeing Fleur again. He even stopped in the bar to knock back a goodbye drink, which was unlike him, but he was feeling a desire for some kind of libation to bless his journey home.

Savouring his gin and tonic (which he'd taken because it was Fleur's drink), he gazed out at the wide corridor, at a clutch of Indian ladies whose billowing saris made them look like colourful frigates, at a group of American ladies on some package tour, at a solemn young man in Muslim robes: all fellow travellers, bound for somewhere. And since he was bound for Fleur, even this ugly building, with its harsh fluorescent lights, seemed lovely to him.

While waiting in the Aer Lingus lounge, he glanced up and, for a moment, thought he was hallucinating. There before him were the O'Driscoll sisters, Nora and Una, both dressed in crisp linen suits, one cream-coloured, the other pale blue, and trundling their luggage along on smart black trolleys. Tony immediately felt sloppy, with his jeans and satchel.

When they glimpsed him, they cried out with delight and hurried over to clasp his hands. Tony could still hardly believe his eyes. They were so utterly of Ballycurry, those two, with their drowsy pub, their singsong accents – how could they possibly be here, in clamorous Kennedy Airport? He gazed fondly at them, marvelling, as always, at their extraordinary looks, Nora's face ornately beautiful, Una's austerely so, despite their age. Spontaneously he tilted down and kissed them both.

They'd been on holiday, they explained excitedly, blushing from the kiss, on holiday in New York for a fortnight, and now they were returning home, to relieve their other sister Cliona, who'd looked after the pub in their absence. When he told them the reason for his own journey, they chorused, "Sorry for your trouble," in the traditional Irish way and grasped his hands again. The word "trouble" reminded Tony of the Troubles in the North, and he suddenly longed to read *The Irish Times* for news of the ceasefire. The American papers carried a paucity of information about any country other than their own, he had realised with dismay during this visit.

But there were no *Irish Times* left on the plane to Dublin; he would have to wait until the Dublin to Cork flight. He also lost sight of the O'Driscoll sisters, then realised they must be flying first-class. What style, he thought admiringly, recalling their *chic* suits and fine luggage. He chastened himself for ever presuming that they were merely timid Irish countrywomen who'd probably never ventured beyond Clonakilty, whereas they were actually much classier travellers than himself.

The short wait in Dublin airport seemed interminable, because at this point he was aching to see Fleur and fatigued from the flight, during which he'd been too excited to sleep. But the view from the window of moist sky, citadels of white cloud and green fields was as soothing to him as a cool drink.

They boarded the Cork plane, and once again he was separated from the O'Driscoll sisters (who were not at all rumpled, and had slept, they said, like babies). Finally he'd be able to read an Irish newspaper. But they didn't have *The Irish Times*, only the *Cork Examiner*, explained the air hostess in a Cork accent, with a slightly stern look, as though it had been gauche of him to even think of requesting that other, that Dublin paper.

"The *Examiner* will be grand," he assured her.

He was so eager for news of the North, his eye nearly missed the article on page one. It was the photograph which finally seized his attention – a colour photograph of his very own valley, those familiar fields beneath a misty sky. Then he read, "Woman Murdered in Glenfern Townland."

Tony had the curious sensation that his arms and legs were turning to water. Breathing rapidly, he read on:

> Gardai are not yet releasing the identity of a woman who was brutally murdered last night in Glenfern, three miles west of Ballycurry, in secluded West Cork.
>
> Officials are stating only that the victim was savagely beaten by her assailant, and that a man is being questioned today in connection with the murder. The State Pathologist arrived on the scene early this morning.
>
> Glenfern is a wide but sparsely populated valley, containing a mere five farmhouses, each about one half mile from its nearest neighbour. Most of these houses have been bought by non-Irish nationals.
>
> The residents of Ballycurry and the nearby resort village of Ballybracken are expressing deep shock in the aftermath of the crime, especially since those areas had become famous for their safety and tranquillity. "We always left our doors open, even when

we went away," declared Seamus O'Sullivan, a
Ballycurry shopkeeper, "but, sure, we won't be so
casual from this day out."

Later, Tony couldn't remember how he survived the remaining twenty minutes or so of that purgatorial flight. Never had the confines of a plane seemed so like a prison. All he wanted was to get there, to be in Glenfern. *It mightn't be Fleur*, he kept repeating to himself, his mind swirling, but the only other woman who lived in their valley was Farmer Coughlan's eighty-year-old sister. *Maybe it was her, maybe someone killed Miss Coughlan*, he consoled himself, guilty that he should wish the poor old woman harm. Not that this possibility comforted him for long, since he was fairly sure that the murderer was Gabriel, and why would Gabriel kill old Miss Coughlan?

He gave a shudder. It had suddenly occurred to him that the murderer might not be Gabriel after all, but Fleur's ex-husband, mad Nicholas York with his womanising and tantrums. Perhaps he'd flown to Ireland, to *reason* with her, and then, when she hadn't been tractable, he'd beaten her to death. Tony fought to keep himself from groaning aloud and alarming his neighbour, a middle-aged man engrossed in a book called *Damage*.

He couldn't stop thinking about how helpless Fleur was during love, about that evening in her apple orchard, how he had remained alert while her composure unravelled beneath his hand. The eagerness of this distinguished woman to abandon herself had always delighted him, but now he was imagining that Gabriel had sensed this quality in her, had known, by the crude oil of instinct, that despite her poise she was vulnerable.

Or if the murderer were indeed Nicholas York, he would be familiar with these intimate things about Fleur.

Tony met Nora and Una on the way out to the car park. He knew he must look peculiar. Without a word, he thrust the newspaper at them.

Una put a hand up to her mouth, and Nora exclaimed, "Holy lamb of divinity!"

Tony found some relief in the simple fact of their distress and their understanding of his own. They offered him a lift, but he said, "I've a hired car. I'll speed along the inland road, which should get me to Glenfern in about an hour and a half."

They did not suggest that he should ring Fleur's house or the police barracks in Ballycurry. It was as though they understood that he must simply get there, that a phone shrilling in an empty house or a garda's neutral voice would be unendurable now. He must simply get there and see for himself.

Ironically, it was one of those perfect Irish summer mornings, all luminous sky, the hedges bright with foxglove. He drove very fast, both hands clutching the wheel, through still-sleeping towns, past the fertile farmland close to Cork city, and then into the rougher, moorlike terrain of West Cork.

Just outside Drimoleague, a garda car stopped him. The policeman was gruff but not unpleasant. "If you'd been driving any faster," he said severely, "you'd have shorn the wool off them poor sheep you were after passing."

"I'm sorry," Tony tried to keep the panic from his voice. "I'm sorry, but I've only just arrived from America, and I learnt about the murder, and I – I live in Glenfern. The woman who was killed – she might be – I'm afraid she might be my girlfriend." He swallowed painfully. "Would *you* know – could you tell me – the victim's name?"

The man gave him a pitying look. "No, lad, I wouldn't know."

Tony was silent, helpless with dread. The garda touched his shoulder. "Drive on, now, but not so fast, for if your friend is safe and sound, wouldn't she be grieving if you were killed in some smash-up!"

As he approached Ballycurry in its hollow and saw the well-loved curve of its road, its houses a coat of many colours, he began to sob and had to stop for a moment to drag a sleeve across his eyes. His Fleur, the flower of his life. And, coward that he was, he had never told her how much he loved her.

The village was still asleep. Tony saw no one there except a man carrying boxes into Seamus O'Sullivan's shop (where, oh God, he had first met her). He had expected agitation, people clustering on the corners, Garda Caffrey moving amongst them, but the silent road bore no evidence of tragedy. He turned right, towards Glenfern.

The hedges were cloudy with emerald fern and pink dog rose. As he pitched along, he glimpsed, for a mere second, a sparrowhawk in the road, bearing down on some quarry, its wings enfolding the smaller bird in an almost tender way. *Bad omen, bad omen*, Tony thought, nearly hysterical now, averting his eyes and grasping the wheel in hands filmed with sweat.

He passed his own house, and, as he barrelled down towards Fleur's drive, he saw a policeman walk out her kitchen door, and then he knew the worst was true.

He felt calm all of a sudden, as though he'd been given a

sedative. It was curiously like being on a beach with a salt wind
in one's ears and people moving in a haze of brine. Time
seemed to stop; he felt nothing. Then he registered two police
cars on the lawn. The garda got into one and began talking into
a mobile phone. He didn't see Tony walk up to the house and
push open the door.

At first the kitchen seemed a sea of blue, although there were
only four policemen there. It was just that they were so broad-
shouldered; and their formidable uniforms, leather and metal,
made them look even larger.

If only I hadn't stayed away so long, Tony lamented wildly to
himself. *If only I'd come home earlier. . .*

The gardai were in a huddle, speaking softly. Then, while
Tony gazed at them, unobserved, one moved slightly, tilting to
confer with the man on his left and creating a chink in the wall
of blue. Through this break Tony saw Fleur, seated on a kitchen
chair, her hands curved round a teacup. When she noticed him,
she said, "Oh, Tony," in a relieved voice and gave him a tired
smile. The policemen turned round in unison, the same look
of wary surprise on all their faces.

To his horror and shame, Tony doubled over and vomited.
Actually, he produced only a flow of bile, since he'd eaten no
dinner on the transatlantic flight, nor, in his anguish, had he
taken breakfast on the plane to Cork.

"Tony!" cried Fleur again, making to rise, but he stumbled
over to her and, under the astonished eyes of the policemen,
collapsed on his knees and buried his head in her lap. He could
not speak; his joy was too fierce. She had come back from the
dead for him.

Chapter 11

GABRIEL HAD FELT like a conquerer, sure of Lottie's return, but she did not come back. She also refused to speak to him on the phone, and, when he exasperatedly went once more to her flat, she wouldn't let him in. Frustrated, he abandoned his resolve to stop drinking. He was constantly furious, and for the first time in his life it occurred to him that rage could be a sickness, tincturing the blood, curdling the stomach. His saliva had turned to acid, and he was afflicted with diarrhoea and paroxysms of coughing. Only when drunk did he attain a measure of peace.

Unable to work (thanks to that castrating bitch, Fleur), he took to staring at the television, a bottle of spirits between his thighs. On the news he learnt of a place called the Garvaghy Road, a tiny Catholic enclave in Northern Protestant Portadown, where the natives were getting restless. After years of enduring Orange parades – shrill fifes, pounding lambegs, triumphalist gear – the Catholics were finally crying, "Why must they march along our road, when they have the whole town? Why must we abide this?" On the other hand, the Orange Order were insisting on their right to free assembly.

At first, Gabriel considered the whole business rather funny. The stone-faced Orangemen with their Laurel-and-Hardy bowlers and their non-existent "culture" were a high-camp scream, while the Nationalists hadn't yet realised that balaclavas and Semtex were a post-modern cliché, terrorist *chic*. But as Gabriel drank and drank (he'd bought a supply of whiskey after leaving Lottie's door the second time), the story began to grow more urgent and personal.

In a bleary way, lolling on his sofa, Gabriel had decided that he was a Unionist; after all, he was Protestant, and he admired their anger. "Fuck you, Gerry Adams," he would shout at the television, or "Keep to your place, fucking Catholics!" while gazing balefully at the Garvaghy Road residents.

As Irish people, North and South, began to fear that this conflict would blight the tenuous ceasefire, the television news programmes grew obsessed with the Garvaghy Road and with the church in Drumcree from which the Orangemen were intending to march. Gabriel listened soggily to interminable discussions, dissections, analyses. One American journalist compared the Garvaghy Road protesters to gay rights activists in Greenwich Village, who had endured years of police savagery before erupting one night in spontaneous protest, thereby changing the course of history. "Fucking homosexuals," muttered Gabriel from his sofa.

Friday morning, he was too sick to keep drinking. Besides, there was no whiskey left. Staggering up from his bed and looking into the bathroom mirror, he was shocked by his face. He forced himself to wash and dress and to take breakfast: strong tea and the last dry pieces of a soda bread he had bought ages ago.

But his rage did not abate. Far from making him feel better, abstinence was tormenting him. Trembling with anger, he lingered at the kitchen table, dipping hard bread into bitter, milkless tea, and thinking about Fleur.

Despite the ague in his body, his head was growing clearer, so that now he could finally understand how outrageous she had been to him. Of course, he had taken refuge in drink: he had merely been trying to protect himself.

The bitch! He clenched his hands into fists on the table. How dare that prim Englishwoman criticise *him*? Why, everyone knew the English couldn't paint. They were a nation of Fleurs, all of them, chill as corpses. No wonder her own paintings were so bloodless. Like all the English, she sheathed herself in aloofness, and like all the English, she paid the price for such brittle self-control. What they forfeited was passion. Ben Nicholson's paintings looked utterly insipid compared to the ardent Americans, to Pollock or de Kooning. Oh, most certainly Fleur Penhalligan would never do anything so vulgar as to *feel*, and God forbid that some emotion should show itself on her static, sterile canvases! Why, she'd be mortified, and her prudish compatriots would be *scandalised, my dear*. God damn her and her precious St Ives School pals. Their genteel pictures were about as exciting as the Sunday watercolours of little old ladies.

Gabriel got up from the table, seized his chair and threw it against the wall. Why had he ever thought that Fleur Penhalligan could give him valuable advice? He knew what *real* art was, far better than she ever would. He was part of a truly vital tradition, a great New York school of painting in which artists were not afraid to be passionate and angry. He could hardly believe that she'd had the gall to lecture him, as though he didn't know what he was up to. After he had successfully weathered the contempt of his family, had it been necessary for her to hurt him in the same way, to trample on the fragile self-confidence that he had barely managed to salvage from his early life?

He went out for a brief walk, noticing nature for the first time in days: drystone walls, spires of foxglove, cream-coloured flowers whose name he did not know. Everything along the hedge was so minute, a living web of leaf, flower and lichen. Gazing along the road, he suddenly imagined Lottie gliding towards him on her blue bicycle. His eyes began to burn, and he turned back.

He prepared a cup of instant coffee, then entered his studio almost gingerly, wanting to paint but afraid. He stared at the picture he'd been working on, a satirical, Beckmann-like study of his parents, both of them scarlet-faced and grimacing, with a foul-looking matter trickling out of their mouths. Only days before he'd been excited by this painting, but now nothing was coming. Anyway, his hands were trembling so violently he couldn't even lay out colours, much less bring brush to canvas.

After cursing Fleur once more, he lay down on the sofa. He had to admit that he missed Lottie dreadfully. She had been a warm presence in this house, keeping it clean and sweet-smelling, leaving him savoury meals and, most crucially, satisfying him sexually. He pictured her full breasts and thighs, her red mouth which he'd liked to bruise with his teeth, and he remembered the smell of her, at once spicy and marine, sharp as coriander.

Groaning, he pressed his face into the cushion and managed to sleep for a while, but it did not refresh him: opening his eyes, he touched his cheeks and found them wet with tears. What was happening? It appalled him to think that Fleur might have plunged him back into an all-too-familiar abyss. He decided immediately that he should walk over to her house, to give her a piece of his mind. His malaise was due to her, so why not have it out with her, tell her the truth about her twee paintings? It might reinvigorate him; besides, let *her* know what it feels like to be put down by an honest critic.

It was later than he'd thought; he must have slept too long. The light in the sky was mellowing, and the birds had started their evening chorus. At one point, he stopped, clutching on to a piece of hedge, and vomited into the ditch. His knees were straw. Still he kept walking.

He opened her kitchen door and strode in. She was standing at the cooker, throwing salt into a pot of something. He noticed that she was wearing jeans and a rather schoolgirlish white blouse, with a round collar. When she saw him she put down the salt cellar and brought a hand up to her chest. "Dear God," she said in a low voice, "you mustn't do that. You mustn't just walk into people's houses."

Without a word he sauntered up to her. She was afraid. He could smell it off her, and this was so satisfying to him, he instantly felt better, as though her fear of him were an elixir.

As he approached, he expected her to back away, but she stood her ground; he had to say that much for her. He had come so close, they were almost touching; he could feel her breath on his face. She was nearly as tall as himself, but not quite, and she was so slim and delicately made, he could easily break her in two. Her wide, honey-coloured eyes were looking coolly at him, but there was a tremor in her body that he could feel from his diminishing distance.

Yet the things he had meant to say to her flew out of his mind. He was aware only of her closeness, of the fear which was spilling from her pores into the air between them, of the fact that it was making him feel much stronger. She had hurt him. No, something more terrible than that. She had invaded the only place in himself that he cherished, his secret grove. She had nearly soiled it, but with this symbolic act of revenge he was cleansing it of her.

Suddenly, while they stared at each other, whatever she had been simmering began to boil over, sputtering down the sides of the pot and into the flames beneath with a venomous, sizzling sound. Without taking her eyes off him, she extended her hand and turned off the cooker.

More and more, he was enjoying this silence between them, her shallow breathing, the sharp smell of her fear. He felt they could stand like this for ever, the magician with his prey caught in a dark spell.

Suddenly she tried to move away, but he grasped her arms and pressed her against the wall. "Let me go," she said in that same low voice. "Let me go, Gabriel."

He smelled her sweat. The illustrious Fleur Penhalligan,

sweating like a pig for fear of him! He could fuck her now, if he pleased, but her frightened face, those alarmed eyes, were all he wanted.

With a laugh, he released her, turned round and walked out.

• • •

His victory called for a celebration. Why, it was as though he had vanquished his father – that cruel voice, that darkness of the heart – had banished the bastard from his life, finally and for good. Freedom! Freedom from Matthew, from Fleur, from his own harsh voices. He strode buoyantly home, his painterly eye noticing the flowers, the stone walls, the robins and butterflies. He would be ready to work again tomorrow and to explore the fields and hills, as he had done when he first arrived in Glenfern, those good days before Fleur.

He got into his car and drove to O'Driscoll's pub. It had entered his mind that Lottie might be there, and now, so exhilarated, he was nearly convinced that he could persuade her to return to him. After all, he was certainly the best thing that had ever happened to her. Why, he would even read her juvenile plays and poetry and offer criticism; under his strict eye she might finally blossom as a writer.

Una and Nora were on holiday in America, explained the lady behind the bar, who introduced herself as their sister Cliona. She had the same large blue eyes as Nora and a similar old-fashioned beauty.

The pub was fairly crowded, and he became aware of quite a few Northern accents. In fact, the youngish man beside him was telling Cliona that he and his family journeyed down from

County Armagh to West Cork every summer, to escape the marching season.

Gabriel, firing back his third double whiskey and calling for a fourth, offered to buy his neighbour another pint.

"Thanks," said the man, proffering his glass in a toast, "*Slainte.*"

"My pleasure," Gabriel answered jovially. Then a pause. "So, tried any kneecapping lately?"

The man's smile vanished, and he pushed his scarcely touched fresh pint away. "Are you saying that you think everyone from the North is a terrorist?"

Gabriel chuckled. "Well, it seems to me that you're all mad, up there: the self-righteous Orangemen and your lot as well, with your atavistic belief in Gaelic superiority. You're as bad as the Nazis. For them it was the Aryans, for you, the Celts. You think being Celtic gives you the right to bomb people to bits. You're all crazy."

The man said quietly, "You are American, aren't you? Do you think, coming here from America, that you are in any position to draw such easy conclusions about our country and our complicated history?"

Gabriel laughed again. "It isn't hard, you know. It's all pretty simple. Both sides are bloody-minded and boring. I suppose you deserve one another." He asked Cliona for yet another whiskey. He was feeling expansive. The world, rinsed of his former gloom, seemed to glow with renewed promise. He extended a hand towards his new pal. "Take your Drumcree-Garvaghy Road business. Nonsense! Northern Ireland is a free country, isn't it? Why can't you allow those people to parade where they please? I would agree that they look ridiculous with those sashes and bowlers, and their music is shit, but surely they cannot be forbidden to march?"

The Northern man answered softly, "The Nationalists are not objecting to the Drumcree march because of the Orangemen's costumes or their music. The truth is that the marches are *meant* to be sectarian; they are essentially an expression of loathing for Catholics, of the desire to eliminate them. And the Orangemen choose to conduct their sectarian march through one of the only Catholic roads in all Portadown. Wouldn't you say that they are being provocative?" He paused. "As you, also, are being?" Again he was silent, then, "Excuse me," he muttered.

Abruptly, he left his place at the bar and walked over to a large family group at one of the tables. After a brief exchange they all stood, abandoning their drinks and gathering up children and bathing things. With a cordial goodbye to the pub at large, they walked out the door. Those who remained stared at their retreating backs. Suddenly the room was silent; after a moment Gabriel noticed that everyone's gaze was on him.

"'Nother whiskey," he commanded.

Cliona looked over his shoulder. "No, boy, you've had enough. Go on home, now."

He was clear-headed enough to feel the silence that continued to encircle him. This place, which only a few moments before had been vibrant with the sounds of summer gaiety – laughter, chatter and the chinking of glasses – was now still as a church. Unabashed, he stared at his fellow patrons, stared them down until they averted their heads. "Lily-livered," he tried to say disdainfully, referring to their middle-class squeamishness, but his tongue had thickened in his mouth, and the word emerged as "Rilly-ivvered". Anyway, they could all go to hell. If this bitch refused to serve him, he would leave her pub with more dignity than any of the local yokels could ever muster.

But his intended swagger faltered to a stagger, and the door handle seemed to blur when he tried to grasp it. Yet somehow he made it out into the road, where the cool night air revived him a bit. It had grown dark, and the whole village was redolent of the steaks being grilled next door at Fiona's Restaurant. Bitterly, Gabriel recalled suggesting to Fleur that she should dine with him there. Well, he mustn't forget that today he had triumphed over her. It was important that he should remember this, so that his elation would not vanish, despite those ignorant wretches in the pub.

The smell of Fiona's steaks was making him ravenous. He walked shakily up to Sweeny's Takeaway and ordered a bag of chips which he devoured in the road. Then, feeling nearly sober again, he got into his car and drove towards home.

Thank God Garda Caffrey didn't seem to be out on patrol; the man was a stickler for law and order, which bored Gabriel profoundly. "Self-important, small-town cop," he muttered now, dismayed that his jubilation of the afternoon had been tarnished, despite himself, by that nasty scene with the Northerner. "They're all rustic ignoramuses," he continued to soliloquise, grasping the wheel and peering ahead as his headlamps scalloped wands of light into the dark road. Some animal, perhaps a fox, glided like mercury across his path and into the hedge.

As he approached his house, he was astonished to see all the lights blazing, as though a party were going on inside.

"Strange," he murmured; on the other hand, he'd been in such a peculiar state since Fleur had reviled his paintings, he might indeed have done something as weird as leaving all the lights turned on in the middle of the day.

But when he got out of the car, his eye fell on Lottie's bicycle, thrown down on the lawn. His heart gave a jump: she had come back! Once again, things were looking up. He could put that unfortunate incident in the pub behind him. While he unbuttoned his jacket, it occurred to him that all through his life envious people had tried to make him feel bad about himself, had tried to loose the voices which could swarm like wasps through his mind. How sick he was of those voices, for ever insisting that he was *no good*, that he had failed *yet again.* But he must not forget that today he'd had a victory. He had neutralised Fleur's venom, deprived her of her power over him. She'd been so terrified – why, she might even have pissed herself, as he had done as a child when his father had frightened him. This notion made him laugh. And, now, Lottie had come back. He moved impatiently through the house, calling her name.

She wasn't downstairs, which made him even more elated. She'd gone up to the bedroom, was probably waiting for him within the sheets, her body warm and eager. She would redeem these recent terrible days. They would make love, he would stop drinking, there would be no more embarrassing scenes in pubs, he would paint again.

He hastened up the stairs, but although the bed-table lamps were burning, the room was empty. He hovered on the threshold. Then he heard a sound from the studio. It was the radio, which he kept there so as to listen to music while painting. Why was she in his studio, she who had always been so indifferent to his work, who seemed to have no visual sense at all?

As he walked along the corridor, he heard a voice reciting the news, more trouble in the North, that riven place, an assassin in some housing estate, a man murdered on his way to work, the wife keening over his body in the road. Gabriel opened the studio door. "Lottie?"

She was standing in the middle of the room, looking flushed and rather beautiful. He registered that she had finally abandoned her jeans and sweater – probably because the summer was so warm – and was wearing, for once, an appealing blue dress with large red buttons down the front. Next he had an impression of a figure in a myth, a goddess or an ancient heroine, and he wondered why this should be so, why her stance should suddenly evoke for him some female warrior, Kali or Athena. Then he saw the kitchen knife clutched in her left hand.

"As the Drumcree march approaches, tensions are mounting to fever pitch," declared the news reader. Gabriel walked over and switched the radio off; he didn't know why, except that in some obscure way he was feeling that there should be silence for what would take place now.

"Lottie?"

She did not answer, only stared at him, breathing heavily. Her dress sported a demure collar – much like the collar of Fleur's white blouse – which curved down to reveal the hollow between her collarbones, gleaming with sweat.

He felt so full of foreboding, the breath was dragging in his chest. Something was telling him to look only at her, that it would be dangerous to look elsewhere. But when once again she did not speak, he walked more fully into the room and glanced about him.

The painting on the easel, the dark study of his parents, had been destroyed, slashed to tatters. Of those against the wall, only one seemed damaged, his favourite Delauney-inspired picture, all shimmering yellows: saffron, pollen, Byzantine-gold, corn-yellow, flax-yellow. She'd cut a ragged wound into the centre of this canvas, but then, apparently, had given up on it, to devote herself with a greater fervour to the one on the easel.

Later, Gabriel would be unable to explain how he felt at that moment of discovering what she had done to him, unable to describe the depth of his pain. She had driven that knife into his heart.

Looking at him, she must have realised that she had gone too far, because she gave a whimper and started to back away. He walked up to her and seized her left arm, twisting it. She cried out, and the knife clattered to the floor.

Her defiant, goddess-like bearing had utterly vanished. Now she was a snared animal, goggle-eyed and trembling. Her skin exuded a musk of fear, and he wondered why this smell was familiar to him until he remembered himself and Fleur in her kitchen earlier that very day.

His voice was calm when he explained what he would do to her. And he was not surprised when she did not protest, when her body sagged in his arms and she merely groaned in response to his measured words. It was as though he had always known this about her, that underneath her surliness she was already

defeated, that beneath her impudence, her seeming compla-
cency, she was secretly resigned to such an outcome as would
befall her tonight. It was as easy as drowning a bag of kittens.
He didn't even know how it was done. One minute he was
looking at the red buttons on her dress, and then, suddenly,
everything was red.

Chapter 12

HIS HEAD STILL in her lap, Tony began to babble, "I shouldn't have gone away. I shouldn't have left you here, unprotected. *I will never, ever leave you again.*"

"Hush," she said, caressing his hair. "Hush, it's all right now."

Before he knew it someone had settled him in a chair, and he was drinking a cup of extremely sweet tea and eating biscuits. With a kind of dreamy bafflement, he looked up at the policemen, who were encircling him as they had surrounded Fleur just minutes ago when he blundered in here. Their faces, tilting over him, were uniformly solicitous, almost maternal, and it amused him to think that it was one of these rugged men who had made tea for him and given him sugary biscuits as though he were a child.

After he'd drunk three cups and eaten about ten biscuits, he was coherent enough to speak and to listen. He explained how he'd read the *Examiner* on the flight, stumbling on an article which had nearly convinced him that Fleur was dead.

"Poor Tony," she murmured, standing next to him with a hand on his shoulder.

"Journalists," growled one of the policemen. "We told them to write *nothing*."

Tony grasped Fleur's hand. "What *has* happened? Who has been murdered?"

Another garda, older than the others, with a grey moustache, recited solemnly, "Just before midnight yesterday, a neighbour of yourself, an American man called Gabriel Phillips, killed a local girl, Charlotte Curran, in his house. We are here at the moment to ask Mrs York a few questions because this Gabriel Phillips threatened her as well, earlier in the day."

Fleur lowered herself heavily into the chair beside Tony. He was still clutching her hand, as though to reassure himself that she was truly there, alive and unharmed. She began to speak in a dull voice, "Where was I? Oh, yes, I turned round and there he was. He'd walked in without announcing himself, and he looked worse than terrible. He was dishevelled and unshaven, and he *stank*." She gave a shaky laugh, her free hand pushing at her hair with the gesture Tony had feared he would never see again.

She went on, "It wasn't just booze he smelled of, although that was part of it; nor was it merely the unpleasant smell of someone who hadn't been keeping himself clean, although that was also part of it. I thought it was his rage that I was smelling, his rage and sickness. He came up to me and grasped me by the arms. He didn't speak. His eyes were red and he looked – and smelled – like a diseased animal. It was then that I sensed this absolute rage in him. He would have thought it was to do with

me, with being insulted by me, since I hadn't praised his pictures. But I myself felt that it had nothing to do with me, or
anyone. It was as though all the ordinary human feelings had
been blasted out of him and he had been diminished, distilled,
to pure rage. As though it was the only passion he could
express, out of all the human passions, if you see what I mean,
the only response he could have. But he didn't say anything,
and neither did I. He must have seen I was afraid." She gave
another uneasy laugh. Tony squeezed her hand. "I suppose my
fear gratified him, because he simply left. He had pushed me up
against the wall, and he seemed quite pleased with himself. I
said, 'Let me go,' or something like that. And then he did. He
dropped his arms and walked out, just like that."

She looked at Tony, her eyes stricken. "I cannot but feel
responsible. You tried to caution me, but, dear God, I didn't
listen. In my folly, my *hubris*, I thought I could talk to him
about *painting*; I think I really believed that I could help him!
But he wasn't interested in painting. As I've said, all emotional
complexity had somehow been blasted out of him. All he could
really feel was fury." She gave a grim laugh. "You tried to teach
me the difference between indulgence and compassion, but I
was too stubborn to hear. I indulged him, to be sure, but I
could not muster enough compassion to realise how extreme
he was or how much he was suffering. And so I loosed it, his
fury. I set it loose, and now he has killed that poor girl."

"Nonsense," interjected the policemen with the grey moustache. "That lad was a time bomb, by all accounts. If you
hadn't agreed to look at his paintings, what would have happened then? He might well have attacked you for your coldness

to him. Or if you'd told him his paintings were masterpieces, just to please him, and then he tried to kiss you and you object-ed? Ah, I'm afraid the only fault is his. Anything could have provoked him."

"What did happen?" Tony repeated in a low voice. "How did he kill her?"

There was a general shuffling of feet; a young, ginger-haired garda coughed. Finally the older policeman spoke bleakly. "He beat her to death." He seemed to hesitate; then continued in the same wintry voice. "Peculiar thing is, she'd brought a knife up there, in his painter's studio where the killing took place. It seems she'd been tearing up his pictures. But your man didn't use the knife. Which is a pity, in a terrible way. What I mean is, it might have made things a bit easier for the girl, faster like. As it was, he took his time. Though when he thought he'd fin-ished her off, he did panic and ring the barracks. 'There's a dead girl here,' he shouted into the phone. But when Chris Caffrey arrived. . . "

The garda took a deep breath. Tony, looking at his haggard face, observed to himself that despite being guards these men were almost certainly not used to violent crime. Drunks pitch-ing home in their cars after hours, cannabis amongst the hip-pies, small-time smuggling in Ballybracken – such had been the extent of villainy in these parts. The policeman who was telling him this unspeakable story was probably as unnerved by it as Fleur and himself.

The garda went on, "When Chris Caffrey arrived, she wasn't yet dead. It took her a while to die. Her mother . . . Perhaps there was some comfort in it for the mother, because the priest said that when he was giving the girl the last rites, she was able to squeeze his hand. Yet another pause. "It seems Phillips used everything he could to pummel her, bits of his own easel, the wooden frames, even a portable radio, to say nothing of his own fists and feet. But he only beat her. He never touched the knife."

"Did he rape her?" asked Fleur, almost whispering.

"No," answered the ginger-haired garda. "There was no sexual assault. Nor did she fight back very much. As though she knew. . ."

"He was so much stronger than her," the older man said, "sure, she knew she hadn't a chance." He placed a broad hand on Fleur's shoulder. "You're a lucky woman, Mrs York. It could just as easily have been your good self."

• • •

When the full story broke on television and in the press, all Ireland was obsessed with it. The elements were at once glamorous and sordid: rich American, local colleen, bucolic Ballycurry defiled by murder, an odour of sex around it all. Yet for all the national interest – the lurid coverage in the Sunday papers – very little prurience prevailed amongst the locals. Sometimes, in the aftermath of scandal, a current trembles through those associated with it, a kind of glow composed of excitement and pleasure, although no one, of course, would admit to such feelings. But the citizens of Ballycurry were not savouring their local tragedy; there were no self-important gossip sessions in the tea shop, no voyeuristic relishing of the latest developments. Everyone was merely upset. All summer lightness vanished. No one exclaimed any more about the splendid weather, music no longer flowed out from the pubs. People moved about the road with heavy faces.

A few reporters attended Lottie's funeral, but they were tactful enough to huddle at the back of the church. Afterwards, Tony and Fleur went to the mother's small farmhouse close to Ballybracken, along with the other mourners.

Nora and Una O'Driscoll had prepared the food, and Lottie's two brothers were circulating through the rooms with bottles of whiskey and wine while their mother remained on a chair in the middle of the kitchen, her hands open on her lap. She was a plump woman, with the same round blue eyes as her daughter. But they looked afflicted now, the skin beneath smudged with purple shadows and the eyes themselves strangely cloudy, as though blurred with cataracts. She barely moved or spoke, and the guests let her be, but for consolations murmured in her ear or a squeeze of her listless shoulder.

Yet at one point she roused herself to speak with Tony, who had come in to offer his condolences. Taking his arm, she said, "You are American? Ah, we lived nine years in America. Lottie was ten when we returned." She was silent a moment, then continued in a rush, "Some are saying that we oughtn't to allow so many foreigners in, that this wouldn't have happened if there weren't so many Americans and English and Germans about. But I don't know. That man who killed my child is just evil, wherever his people come from. Sure, we in our family always liked talking with the Americans who come to Ballybracken. And Lottie quite liked living in the States. She cried when we came back. Ach, she was a fat little thing, with curls so thick I cropped them off, they were that hard to put a comb through. Lately she was wearing her hair long, though I told her it would only tangle and make her look streelish . . ." She stopped suddenly, her mouth open. It was clear she had forgotten for a second that Lottie was dead. Then she resumed more slowly, "She was a happy child, I think, though always quiet-like, as though she had a secret. I used wonder had something happened once, some bad thing, which she was afraid to speak of . . ."

Her hand dropped from Tony's arm. Staring with those grief-occluded eyes into the distance, she murmured, "I am only half alive now. I think I will never be whole again. It isn't like when my husband died, God bless him. His was a natural death." She paused once more. Tony waited beside her, his heart breaking for Lottie and for his own father. When she spoke again, her voice was so soft that he had to tilt towards her. "I should have asked her. I should have asked her about the bad thing which might have happened when she was small. Perhaps it was her dad. He was a bit strict with her, now and again, but only for her own good, of course. She was always so lonely. But she did admire her new employer, that Mr Phillips, that monster who killed her. He was so handsome, she said, like an American film star."

• • •

The marching season went on, the Orangemen continuing to parade throughout the beleaguered North. In Ballycurry, people were still depressed. Their place had been blighted by a horror so unutterable, it lay like a foul smoke on the air. How could they cleanse themselves, how could they continue to pass the flat where she had lived, to speak with their neighbours about weather and the harvest, to go to market and work, after such a soiling?

They were angry, many of them, without knowing it. This Gabriel, this rich foreigner, had desecrated their home place. He would have no idea what this region meant to the people whose families had lived here for centuries, whose blood coursed through this earth like the channels of copper which their ancestors had mined and which still coloured the rivers brown. The old villages of Ballycurry and Ballybracken were freighted with human history. Catholics and Protestants alike had sickened and died here in the famine; children who had perished then were buried all along the fields of Glenfern. The name of each townland, each mountain, each stream had evolved from the Irish. For the old people, certain trees, certain rivers, paths and pastures were graven on their hearts. But now this stranger had transformed their home area into a valley of gloom.

There was a thickening murmur, a groundswell of hatred for Gabriel, which did not abate over time but deepened. Many began to declare that he should be extradited to America for his punishment. What they really meant by this was that they wanted him to receive the death penalty.

Tony was surprised by how alarmed he felt by this response amongst the locals, their thirst for vengeance. It seemed to him almost an echo of the belligerence which continued to throb southwards from those Orange marches; it contained a similar dearth of pity, a similar acrid smell, fire and brimstone.

Which is not to say that Tony felt pity for Gabriel. Quite the opposite. When he thought of how that man had killed Lottie and how he'd tried to terrify Fleur, he literally shook with loathing. But, *We should try to have pity*, he said to himself one day, in an effort to understand his own feelings, *We should try to summon pity. Not for Gabriel, but for ourselves.*

What did he mean by this? He didn't know. But he pictured a tree thronged with carrion birds, and jackals circling round the house of a dying man, howling for blood. He pictured an Aztec temple, the victim lying beneath a grimacing frieze while smoke eddies into the sky. He pictured heretics being drawn and quartered in Tyburn. He remembered that story he had read in New York, about the young boy who had killed his grandfather: *Fry him.*

How many centuries had passed since Apollo exhorted Orestes to slaughter his own mother, exacting from him the blood sacrifice, imprisoning him in a cycle of vengeance? Finally Athene released Orestes from that halter of vengeance, introduced him and all Athens to the idea of justice; but now, certainly, after so many aeons fouled with human blood, a further progress could be made, from justice to mercy?

Walking through the summer fields or lying sleepless beside Fleur at night, Tony tried to understand what he himself meant by *mercy*. He knew that if he tried to explain it, people would recoil from him, as though he were declaring that Gabriel should be cosseted. No, he couldn't describe it yet, not even to Fleur; it was still merely a series of images, the hedges swathed in that dawn gossamer, the Aztec temple, the carrion beasts screaming for blood.

He remembered something Fleur had told him, about how we disliked Gabriel because his stridency reminded us of our own desperation. Tony wondered what he himself might have become if, like Gabriel, some early trauma had made him unable to grow as an artist. Might he also have become bitter and arrogant? Was there not a potential Gabriel in each one of us? Not that we were all incipient murderers, but certainly a narcissistically injured child remains a part of every adult's psyche. So when the people of Ballycurry muttered, *Send him back, so that he might be put to death*, what could they not bear, what did they want not to see? He began to realise that the fact of mercy was this: once you felt it, you could no longer cease to care. You could no longer reduce people to something less than human, as Gabriel Phillips had done, and as some townsfolk would wish to do to him.

Tony recognised that if you did succeed in crushing your own capacity for mercy, it was your own humanity which you imperiled. Executing people was like looking at some dark thing with loathing, and then becoming it, becoming the very darkness you beheld.

When Gabriel was tried, his parents were not present. His mother finally appeared on television, after Irish reporters flew to New York and stalked her for days. "I have no son," was all she said, with a frigid smile. Considering the circumstances, Tony thought she looked monstrously unruffled. The father did not appear before the cameras, refused to speak to the press. In the papers and on television, reporters described this couple as "stony" or "cold". Yet they were also "fantastically wealthy", and had given their son "every advantage". What, then, had gone wrong? Had their perhaps unnatural coldness deformed their son? Were there dark secrets in Gabriel's past which we would never learn? Was he simply born evil? One of his sisters, a pampered-looking blonde currently in residence in West Cork at her summer home near Castletownshend, also chose not to speak to the press, attend the trial or contact her brother. He was left alone with himself and with his new-found fame. He, who had always wanted to be famous.

Continuing to think about ancient stories, Tony considered how God had stayed Abraham's hand. No more human sacrifice! On the other hand, that same God had let his own son die slowly beneath a pitiless sky. *But surely that was meant to be the last sacrifice?*

Tony was understanding more and more each day. He even dared speak about it. He and Fleur had decided to splurge and dine out at Fiona's Restaurant; they needed a break from the sorrow of that period. It was a lovely meal at a table warm with candlelight. And they discovered that it was soothing to be encircled by tourists rosy with wine, speaking in an array of languages; they seemed so innocent.

Afterwards he and Fleur went to Una and Nora's for a brandy. It was there that the subject of Gabriel's punishment came up, with their classicist friend Aubrey Bellowes.

"Hello, you two," he greeted them, extending his glass. "Terrible, what's happening in the North, isn't it? Reminds one of the *Oresteia*. Immemorial blood feuds and so on. Quite primitive."

Tony said, "I was also thinking about Orestes lately, in another context: how those plays are about replacing vengeance with justice. It was in the context of Gabriel Phillips that I was thinking about them." It was hard for him to utter the name, and he could tell that it was hard for Aubrey and Fleur to hear it in this sociable atmosphere. Fleur stiffened a bit, and Aubrey began elaborately to light his pipe. There was a brief silence. Fleur squeezed Tony's hand.

Then Aubrey said thoughtfully, "There would be a desire for vengeance, of course, amongst the Ballycurrians. They *knew* that wretched child, knew her family." He looked sharply at Tony. "Have people been . . . hostile to you? You being a compatriot of the murderer?"

"No," answered Tony honestly. "Surprisingly enough, no one has been. People are generally just grief-stricken. But the Irish people I met before all this happened were almost universally against capital punishment. They were scandalised that out of all the first world countries, only the States continued to sanction such a beastly thing as executions. When I was living in Dublin, my Irish friends would sometimes talk about the horror of it: the botched jobs, the killing of innocents, the fact that most of those executed are black or poor. So I was surprised when people here began to suggest that maybe Phillips should be extradited, because he could be condemned to death in New York. It shocked me, and I wasn't sure why. I mean, I myself have no sympathy for him."

"The *Oresteia* is also about the Furies," observed Aubrey, "how they shriek for revenge. At the conclusion of the trilogy, they are appeased, of course, but not destroyed." He savoured his pipe for a moment. "I suppose one must consider what would happen to us all, to society, if we loosed the Furies upon anyone, even a murderer."

Tony looked at Fleur, who smiled at him. He noticed that her serious eyes were the same tawny colour as the brandy in her glass. He still marvelled to himself that she was alive; every now and again he would touch her hair, almost shyly, or press her hand to his cheek in a kind of gratitude. He would never

forget the ordeal of driving to her house that morning, his heart
black with fear. Now he said to Aubrey, "I'm remembering our
discussion of a while ago, about Odysseus and the dark side of
our natures. Once, I confided in Fleur that I was sometimes
afraid of my own dark side, of the impulses which I thought
might be wicked or wrong."

He turned to Fleur. "Do you remember? You said the same
thing as Aubrey, that you believed it isn't dangerous to explore
our dark side, so long as it's done in an effort to become more
conscious."

She gave him a warm look, and something quivered between
them.

"It isn't only not dangerous to explore the dark side,"
answered Aubrey emphatically, "it is our responsibility to do so.
It is the only way we become capable of compassion. If we try
to evade our own darkness, we cannot know ourselves, nor can
we feel sympathy for others. We must recognise ourselves, our
own potential, in the vilest of creatures. Only then can we overcome our own vileness." He took a distracted swallow of his
brandy. "People who countenance the death penalty are averting their eyes from their own darker side. 'Kill!' they cry, but it
seems to me that we must honour the god who governs darkness. It is not all black and concealing. Indeed, *daylight* con-
ceals certain mysteries, blanches them, until darkness reveals
them. Like passion." He regarded them closely. "What I mean
is, darkness is kindling, it is what light is born out of, the
unknowing womb from which knowledge is born. Not to say
art." He gave a brief laugh, as though to leaven the gravity of
his words. "Anyway, if we don't try to understand our shadow

side, it takes us over, as it did Gabriel Phillips. No, I have come to realise that one must shake hands with the dark side, if one wishes to be responsible and loving."

He paused, then continued more slowly, "Once, I saw the other side, a rather sensitive side, of our Mr Phillips. It was right here and not too long ago at that. I had recently returned from a visit to the stone circle at Dunbeacon, and we fell into a discussion of ancient places, how enclosed and numinous they can feel, how beyond time. He spoke enthusiastically about Loughcrew and Knockmany and that big dolmen in Clare, called the Pool of Sorrow, places he had read about and longed to see. He was nearly humble, quite unlike himself. Well, I don't suppose he will visit any of those places now, poor tormented creature; his will be a different kind of enclosure from now on."

The pub was growing more crowded. Once again, Fleur squeezed Tony's hand. He felt that she was deeply tired, that her encounters with Gabriel had frightened her so badly she was exhausted still by her effort to recover from them. It was as though some quotidian safety had been torn away, and from now on she would always feel a little bit in danger. The day before, she had turned the television on to see the news. It was noon, and the Angelus bell was tolling behind a particularly beautiful Madonna and Child, a Greek ikon. The Virgin, severe and lovely, was gazing at the baby in her lap, who returned her sombre regard. Standing before the television while the Angelus rang and that Virgin and Child stared at each other, Fleur had started to cry. Tony, who had been about to leave for his own studio, took her in his arms instead and stayed

with her all that day. And then, last night, he had finally told
her the thing which he'd been yearning to say.

"Fleur," he'd begun softly, combing her hair with his fingers,
and spreading it out on the pillow, "your hair is so fair, so
golden."

"Thank you, you romantic lunatic, but it is actually a bit
grey," she had murmured, half-asleep.

"One day it will be entirely grey. One day it will be golden
no longer."

She had turned over and looked at him. "Will you mind
that?"

He'd laughed. "I don't know. I might mind, though I don't
think so. Anyway, I will be here to see it. I will be here through
all the changes, each and every one. We will go through them
together."

Now Aubrey polished off his cognac and said good night.
Tony and Fleur lingered for a while, slowly finishing their own
brandies, and observing their fellow drinkers, many of whom
spoke in the twanging accents of the North. This compelled
Tony to discuss the ceasefire with her: would it collapse?

"I hope it lasts, but I don't think it will," sighed Fleur,
putting her head on his shoulder. "We will last, I think. You
and me. We will try to be constant and true to each other.
Maybe that's the best we can do. Maybe loving and being loved
and looking after the people who belong to us through love,
maybe that is as much as we can do."

"It's no mean thing," Tony answered.

They fired back the last of their brandy and went out, arm
in arm, into the darkness of the road.

Epilogue

February, 1996

As far as Gabriel was concerned, it was he who had been killed. The last ember of natural love had died in his heart with Lottie's death; she had dealt him that blow: the ultimate victory was hers.

He had tried to explain some of this in the courtroom. He had spoken of that night in the studio, how she had shorn him of power even as Samson had been shorn by a woman, how her destruction of his paintings was the first violence, well before he lay a hand on her. He explained that she had killed the last glimmer of love within himself. He had already lost the commonplace refuge of a mother's love, and he had lost his father and sisters as well. But it was Lottie who had removed the last sanctuary, she who had deprived his orphaned spirit of its final hope. He had tried to explain to the court that what he'd felt in that room, before he attacked her, was a sense of loss so unspeakable, it was nearly as though he were dead. He was lost, all promise of redemption gone, and it was her fault.

• • •

In February of the following year, the IRA ceasefire collapsed with the Canary Wharf bombing. People were once again bitter, afraid, depressed. Even in this grey prison, so remote from the North, the men walked about looking dejected.

All except Gabriel, who was taken up with other things. They let him have newspapers – new and old – and he had fallen into the habit (actually more an obsession) of reading about his own trial and conviction. He contemplated the photographs of himself in which he looked romantically hollow-cheeked and wild-eyed, and he read and reread all the accounts, analyses, interviews, the sensational descriptions in the Sunday colour supplements, the more restrained pieces in *The Irish Times*.

A fact which had escaped him during the trial was that Lottie was pregnant when she died. How was it that this had not registered with him? How could he not have heard something so important? Yet it seemed that he had indeed missed that morsel of crucial information, for when he read about it in the papers he was shocked.

The truth was, he missed her. In this place with its stink of toilets only faintly concealed by the stink of disinfectant, with its sunless corridors, watery stews, crushing routines – in this hellish place he had begun again to miss her. He remembered something which at the time had not impressed him. It was only a look he was remembering, a way she had of examining him with a tentative, almost shy expression, underneath her customary sullen air. Why had he not acknowledged it while she was still alive, that look of hers which was hopeful, even appealing, a look which had passed over her face like a breeze ruffling water, and which, he supposed, he had been privileged to see, if he had only known it? Why, it might even have been the limpid look of a soon-to-be mother, trying to find the right moment to inform the lucky man.

It occurred to him that he had loved her. Perhaps. Or something close to love, as close as he could come, anyway. But he had killed it; or, on second thought, surely it was she who had killed it, with her silence. Oh, why had she not told him?

Another, smaller irony had begun to haunt him: simply that she had kept his house so clean and had cooked him such lovely little meals, while she herself had not been clean about her person and had seemed to live on chips and beer. Had she so disliked herself that she would look after him almost tenderly, yet neglect her own basic needs so sorely?

Whatever she had felt about herself, he concluded that she must not have loved him after all, or she would have spoken about the baby. If she'd lived, she would probably have insisted that he marry her, or else he would have had to buy her off. Probably the child wasn't even his! She was full of guile, he consoled himself, and certainly she would have used the baby to exploit him. Yet he thought about her…

By and by he abandoned his ritual of reading the newspaper articles about himself, since he'd memorised them all and no one was writing any new ones. He supposed the world was forgetting about him, but he could not forget the world. Always he thought of Lottie and of Ballycurry, which he'd hoped might become his new home. He had foolishly thought he would be

loved there. Gabriel saw himself as a kind of pilgrim, divested
of mother-love, father-love, looking for a place whose name he
had forgotten. He had thought Ballycurry might be that place,
but they had misunderstood him there. He should have known
that a small town would be full of small-minded people.

Why had they rejected him? And why had Lottie made him
do those terrible things? He supposed they would never understand him. His talent and achievement were beyond their ken.
They would only blame him, make him their scapegoat.

One cold February morning when the prison grounds were
silvered with frost, a letter arrived which changed his life. He'd
had no visitors since he came to this place, except, surprisingly, his sister Alexandra, who'd been in Ireland anyway, staying
with Maeve at her summer mansion. Only Alex had ever
understood the real nature of their family life, the bestiality
beneath the surface, and during her visit here she had alluded
to this. "I tried to protect you, Gabriel," she said feebly, giving
him an anxious look, "but I was only small myself. I'm sorry."

"It doesn't matter," he'd answered, and then she had left,
with a mumbled goodbye, since there was nothing more to say.

He'd had letters from crackpots, informing him that he was
bound for hell, and one letter from a Satan-worshipping
seventy-year-old Galwegian woman, proposing marriage. But
even such loony missives had eventually ceased, and he received
nothing all winter and spring, until that February morning.

It was from a fashionable New York gallery, in SoHo, declaring that they would like to arrange an exhibition of his paintings, including the ones which Lottie had slashed. The gallery
owner sympathised with Gabriel's plight, explaining that the

systems of ethics and morality which defined ordinary people's lives should not govern the lives of artists. The gallery intend- ed to celebrate Gabriel's daring "conceptions", a term which made Gabriel wince. Yet generally he was exuberant. Let the Fleur Penhalligans and Tony Dalys have their meagre triumphs in London or Dublin. He, Gabriel Phillips, was about to con- quer downtown New York, the centre of the art world.